T0348823

ANIMAL

Advance Praise

"Alan Fishbone occasionally conjures the Roman poet Catullus (amid many subjects), and like that great role model he's unafraid to explore the messy effluvia of life: wet coffee grounds on a wall, excreta, the smell of a musky goat. He's also not afraid to explore the pain of betrayal. His voice in this collection of edgy, gritty encounters with life is interspersed with that of his scarred German friend, Dieter, to form a jangling, modernist counterpoint that's highly addictive."

– James Romm, author of *The Sacred Band: Three Hundred Theban Lovers Fighting to Save Greek Freedom*

"A devilish double pour of modern grit and love of antiquity, Alan Fishbone's *Animal* is honest, fearless, and stunningly inventive."

– Daniel Magariel, author of *Walk the Darkness Down*

"Boldly experimental in form, yet with enough narrative drive to hold the reader's attention, *Animal: Notes from a Labyrinth* is a refreshingly challenging read. Author Alan Fishbone's metatextual, frequently scatological novella will linger long in the memory of those bold enough to enter its labyrinth."

– *IndieReader*

"Part novel, part essay, part travelogue of trips to Europe, New York, and South America, the book is also a letter addressed to Fishbone's lover, referred to as 'you.' The writer looks into his own soul with brutal, crude honesty and asks the same of 'you.' Toggling between erudition and sexual fetishes and violence, the narrative is hard to stomach, beautiful, forgiving, and tender in equal measure, much the same way as looking in a mirror is liable to feel. Fishbone's work is a courageous, curious, and experimental example for 'you' to follow."

– Mari Carlson, *U.S. Review of Books*

ANIMAL

Notes from a Labyrinth

ALAN FISHBONE

UNBOUNDED CREATIVITY

HERESY
PRESS

FEARLESS EXPRESSION

Heresy Press books may be purchased in bulk at special discounts for sales promotion, corporate gifts, fund-raising, or educational purposes. Special editions can also be created to specifications. For details, contact the Special Sales Department, Skyhorse Publishing, 307 West 36th Street, 11th Floor, New York, NY 10018 or info@skyhorsepublishing.com.

Skyhorse Publishing® is a registered trademark of Skyhorse Publishing, Inc.®, a Delaware corporation.

Visit our website at skyhorsepublishing.com.

HERESY PRESS
P.O. Box 425201
Cambridge, MA 02142
heresy-press.com

Heresy Press is an imprint of Skyhorse Publishing.

10 9 8 7 6 5 4 3 2 1

Library of Congress Cataloging-in-Publication Data is available on file.

Jacket design by Elizabeth Cline

Hardcover ISBN: 978-1-949846-69-0
Ebook ISBN: 978-1-949846-70-6

Printed in the United States of America

Tragedy is when I cut my finger.

Comedy is when you fall into an open sewer and die.

– Mel Brooks

FINGERIS AD RECTUM

– Horace

I

Begin in Berlin, with insomnia. I hadn't slept for days, just lay there staring into the dark and listening to my ears ring, wishing I could turn off for a while, but that's the thing with insomnia: the more frayed and exhausted you get, the more wired and awake. On the fourth morning, I dragged myself into the kitchen like a zombie, gasping and ravenous for coffee. The coffee machine was one of those screw-together two-piece mechanical espresso jobs, water on the bottom, coffee in the middle, collection chamber on top, a miniature steam engine. I filled it, turned on the stove, and sat down in an empty stupor. The wall seemed to dematerialize into a field of yellow pastel. At some point I realized the pot was gurgling, but when I went to pour a cup, it turned out I'd forgotten to put in the coffee, so the can was full of a jaundiced hot broth like something bled from an old radiator. It seemed to sum up my life at that moment. I should have just sat there and drank it.

For reasons unknown to me, since the apartment was a sublet and I'd never met the owner, there was a second coffee maker of the same type on a shelf above the sink. It was a bit more elaborate, with a handle and knob made of blond wood and a heavier, pedestal-like base that annoyed me. The machine seemed pretentious, a little over-designed, as if it were posing. I'd never used it, but now, since the other one was hot, I took this one down, filled it with water and coffee this time, screwed it together and set it on the stove to brew. Again I sat down. While waiting, I reached for the tarot deck that sat on the kitchen table. Time for the daily prognostication. I shuffled the cards and out popped the Devil card, number XV of the major arcana, in this deck depicted as a long-haired billy goat with flaming hooves and an inverted pentagram inscribed in the center of his horned forehead. He leered out with one malevolent eye from a gloomy gray background. Damn. The deck came with a little manual that explained the cards:

> The Devil. Addiction, Negativity. XV
> Though it may feel frightening when the devil appears in your reading, this card carries an urgent message and must be interpreted with total honesty. The darkness of the devil card takes the form of addiction, negativity, or materialism. It can indicate an ugly relationship with a person or a substance. Identify this dependency and know how it is holding you back. The devil's hooves are strong and relentless. Their grip will not loosen until a conscious decision is made. Free Yourself.

I was pondering that when, with a sudden, strangely undramatic POP, the coffee pot exploded, jetting a scalding wet mud of coffee grounds in every direction, splattering me and all four walls of the kitchen with speckled, wet brown stains. It looked as if some malignant troll had sprayed the whole place with hot, gritty diarrhea. Shit! The kitchen was trashed, and I had to be out of the apartment in three days. The owner didn't even know I was there. A friend of mine had sublet it and had to leave early, so she lent it to me, asking me just "be careful." No problem, I'd assured her; what could happen? She still had a thousand-euro security deposit riding. By now, the first pot was cool, so I picked it up, filled it one more time, then sat back down with my face and hair full of mud to wait for that goddamned cup of coffee.

II

I was drinking the coffee and picking stray grounds from my beard and hair, groggily searching the internet for ways to clean the walls. According to my research, I just had to find a Mr. Clean Magic Eraser, which would whisk the coffee stains off the walls like nothing. Numerous cleaning bloggers were on record as to the eraser's amazing properties, and the corporate blurb was compelling. "To discover the cleaning possibilities, simply take a swipe. Its water activated micro-scrubbers reach into the surface grooves, lifting away built-up grease and soap scum ... Before long, you'll be back to the things you love in a brighter, cleaner space." That was what I wanted: back to the things I loved in a brighter, cleaner space. Like a kind of miniature salvation.

In Germany, Mr. Clean, with his white eyebrows and earring, was called Meister Proper, and the magic eraser a

Schmutzradierer, or "dirt eraser." Already my expectations
were diminishing; no magic, and Mr. Clean under an uptight
alias. He didn't sound like a get-the-job-done-type gangster
anymore. More like some anal-compulsive accountant. And
the Schmutzradierer turned out to be totally ineffective against
the coffee stains. Apparently, they were too ingrained in the
wall for the micro-scrubbers to reach in and lift them away. So
it looked like I would have to repaint the room, and time was
running short.

My next stop was the Bauhaus, a hardware superstore, where
I explained in my limited German to an officious, Himmler-
like man at the paint counter how my coffee machine had exploded, and Meister Proper failed me. He was wearing a white
lab coat and looked at me through his spectacles with a mixture of sympathy and disapproval that I had come to think of
as the national emotion of Germany. He clicked his tongue
and shook his head. How could I have been so naive as to
think that a mere sponge could remove coffee stains? First, he
informed me, I would have to paint over the stains with a thick
and toxic base layer or the stains would re-emerge through
whatever else I put over them, no matter how many coats I
might try. Even this base could require two coats and each one
a full day to dry. And furthermore, he intoned, this stuff was
poisonous, very bad. I must not even think of using it without
correct ventilation. I must open every window in the house.
Did I understand? He said all of this in a low, authoritative
murmur, with apparently little confidence that I would understand, like a trainer trying to teach a dog to play chess. Fuck

him, I thought. I bought what I needed and went home. But Himmler was right. After a few hours applying the base coat in bad ventilation, I had to get out of the apartment. The fumes were giving me a headache and making me dizzy at the same time. So I headed down to the Trinkteufel to have a beer and think things over.

III

Sitting again in the Trinkteufel, which means "Drink Devil" in German, staring down into a glass mug of beer, a ring of white foam fringing the yellow liquid like cobwebs. It looks like the piss it will become, I thought, maybe I'm drinking piss, cycling beer into urine at the rate of roughly six euros an hour. Couldn't I just pee into my own mouth and save myself the trouble? Man walks into a bar ...

The last time I'd been in this place, a couple of days disappeared. I blacked out and woke up in a freezing wooden caravan parked in a dirt lot near Goerlitzer Park. My fingernails were painted dark green, and my beard was stiff with a strange crust. A large form was snoring next to me, hidden under a pile of blankets and clothing. I slipped out without investigating further. I later realized I'd been unconscious for thirty-six hours. Perhaps I'd been drugged and abducted by a yeti?

The bar hadn't changed much. A large gold skull with a pair of spindly antlers hung above the bar like a trophy moose head. Dozens of other skeleton and skull knick-knacks dangled from the walls and ceiling, giving the place the feel of a permanent Halloween party in an underworld rivered with booze. German metal swirled at low volume through the blue, cigarette-fogged air. It was about three in the afternoon.

The door swung open, and a pair of stocky, bald punks stumbled in with a matted gray dog at the end of a rope. Dressed in black, with massive skulls and meaty faces, tattooed hands and necks, rings and studs lining ear, eyebrow, lip, and nostril. They sat down to my left and ordered rum and Cokes in that classic German baritone that seems to come from somewhere behind the sternum, well below the vocal cords, rumbling from depths of tracheal mud and viscera. The Coke must be Coca-Cola Zero, they specified, perhaps for a tinge of nihilistic symbolism. They didn't seem to be dieting. Shots of green Chartreuse as well, a viscous perfume served in miniature martini glasses which they knocked back immediately, pinkies raised daintily high in the air, then lit cigarettes and resumed their conversation about the band S.O.S., drei mal kurz, drei mal lang, drei mal kurz. Save Our Souls. Two men walk into a bar …

More people drifted in, mostly dressed in black. A fat albino-pale girl with purple hair, jumbo safety pin crosswise through her nose like a bone. A Turk with a thick moustache and a few days' beard coating his sallow cheeks. The two to my left kept at it. In the space of half an hour, they drank three rum and Cokes and shots while their dog lay listless on the floor like a heap of filthy rags. Quickly hammered, one, now standing and swaying slightly on his feet, calls the other, "Du, Arschloch!" You asshole! They both laugh, a gravelly, mucus-shuffling laugh that explodes into a classic smoker's hack, wheezing and sputtering. The one standing bends over and coughs so hard I almost expected to see a lung come bubbling out of his mouth. But he rights himself, pink-faced and gasping, and orders another round. Something about the bar and the coughing punk reminded me of a joke, like a biker tattoo come alive: a skeleton walks into a bar and says gimme a beer and a mop.

I felt a tap on my shoulder.

"Hast du Feuer, Mann?" I heard.

I turned my head without looking up and saw a pair of vintage ostrich-skin cowboy boots, pointed and pimpled with quill stumps, a worn-out, scuffled black verging into gray. I looked up and took in the rest of him: a threadbare gray suit jacket over a darker gray hoodie bearing the skull and crossbones logo of the St. Pauli football team, the hood rumpled and bunched at the back of his neck. The head was clean-shaven, almost entirely hairless except for two tufts of white or gray or blond hair parked like a pair of caterpillars above nervous blue eyes. He looked at me expectantly.

"I got fire," I said. "You got a smoke?" I handed him a box of matches that sat in front of me on the bar.

"Ja, man. Where there's fire there's smoke. Don't you Americans say this?"

"Yeah, but usually the other way around."

"I know, but these days everything is backwards, no? The cart is in front of the horse."

"OK. I'm Alan."

"Dieter. *Danke*."

Dieter sat down on the stool next to me and fished two cigarettes from a crumpled blue pack reading NIL on its front in white block letters. *Nothing* in Latin. A brand of cigarettes called nothing. Seemed appropriate. He handed me one as the bartender came over, a short, wiry punk of about fifty with platinum hair glued up and out in radiant spokes like a halo.

"Doppel Vodka, Mann, kein Eis," said Dieter.

The bartender brought back his drink and set it on the bar. It looked like a glass of water.

"Prost," Dieter said. We clinked glasses. He lifted his to his mouth, drained it in one throat-bobbling slug and immediately called for another, then lit our cigarettes, sucking at his like a condemned man awaiting execution. His eyelids closed and flickered as the cigarette ember throbbed red and crept up toward the filter.

"My father just died, man," he exhaled, a mixture of smoke and words, "ninety-four fucking years old. Well, it was a couple of weeks ago, but that's still now, right? I thought that old Kackwurst was going to live forever. Just keep getting more dry until he disappears into a pile of shit and ashes."

"Oh. Sorry to hear that," I said, blandly. I didn't know what else to say.

"Ja. No big deal, man. No pain. I didn't talk to him for like twenty years. He was a mean old guy. Like five people showed up to his funeral, and one of them was the postman, probably because he gave him a schnapps on his birthday. You believe that? Whatever, man, you die like you live. He was a miserable old Nazi douche bag. I love this word 'douche bag.'" He said it again, puckering his lips as he savored the word.

"Wow. I never heard anyone say that here about his own family before. But I guess it must be true of some people, no?"

"Not some people. Everybody my age, man. If not their father, then their grandfather or their uncle. We all have dead bodies in the basement. But who gives a shit? I'm sick of it."

His second drink arrived.

"What? Dead bodies in the basement? You mean like that cannibal guy? I didn't know it was so common."

"Oh, no. It's just a saying. It means like to have a dirty secret. Like papa was a Nazi. Opening a can of worms, maybe?"

"Oh, yeah. No. We say to have a skeleton in the closet. The can of worms is something else. A skeleton in the closet is the dirty secret one. How is it in German?"

"Eine Leiche im Keller haben. *Leiche* is a dead body. Except, here sometimes it's really true, man, like our national cannibal guy you said, but he had his Leiche in the freezer, not a fucking metaphor. He was making schnitzels out of the guy's ass, 300 grams at a time, weighing the pieces for his diet. Germany, man, so fucked up. Everything looks so normal, but it's all bullshit. Germany is like a strict, asshole schoolteacher—everything proper and rules—then at night he goes out like a transvestite and wants to get beaten and shit on, and a fucking zucchini stuck in his ass. To me this is Germany and

Europe, man. One overeducated queer guy eating another one in a big, rotting house. This was even the name of the town. Rottenburg."

"Well, America's no paradise either, man. Don't feel too bad. Actually, I think Germans and Americans have a lot in common. Slavery, genocide, hot dogs. We had our own cannibal too. Not quite as refined as your guy, but still. Did you hear about that?"

"No, man. Really?"

"Yeah, in Florida. But like I said, very different from your guy. No classical music and Shiraz. This was way more violent and sudden. He took some bad drugs, something called 'bath salts.' Well, that's what the cops said. Maybe drugs weren't involved at all, but it's more reassuring to think that than that people just spontaneously explode into rabid cannibal zombies. Anyway, guy gets into his car to go home, and it wouldn't start. He flips out and abandons the car, starts walking along the highway. In Florida, during the hottest part of the day, when anyone who can is hiding out in air-conditioning. Or at the beach. No other way. That heat will make your ears ring. He strips his clothes off, one piece at a time, throwing them away until he's completely naked, still walking along the road with a Bible in his hand and screaming obscenities. Then he starts ripping up the Bible and throwing it around like confetti. Guess he's having a bad day. A couple of alarmed motorists call it in to the cops, but they're a little slow to respond. Understandably. At this point it's just some naked tramp ripping up a Bible on the highway. No big deal, right? You can imagine them thinking let the fucking idiot sunburn his black ass for a while before they get off their own fat, white ones. But then he runs across some old, white homeless guy near a parking lot building where he's been sleeping. Homeless guy's about sixty-five, with scruffy white hair and a beard. It's like a movie. Two guys just walking past each other in this empty American strip-mall landscape with the blinding sunlight splashing white off everything. Nobody else around. Then, all of a sudden, the naked one pounces on the other one, starts pummeling the hell out of him, knocks him to the ground and strips HIS clothes off, so now they're both naked. Then he bites into the guy's face. Bites a chunk of his cheek off, chews it up and fucking eats it. Keeps biting pieces off and chewing them. He's eating the guy's face! Can you believe that? Straight out of the newspaper, the *Miami Herald*, and all over the internet. Somebody saw it and called the cops and finally one shows up, but not before he's chewed half the man's face off, including both his eyes. How the fuck do you bite out someone's eyes? The cop pulls his gun and yells 'Freeze!' The guy looks up with a mouth full of dribbling blood and meat, snarls like an animal, and goes right back to feeding on the victim's head. So the cop shot him, five bullets, killed him instantly. The homeless guy survived, but he's blind and most of his face is gone. Paper said, 'eighty percent of his face above the beard.' I guess the beard didn't taste good. He's going to need a full face transplant. The biggest problem was to keep his head from getting infected. A doctor they consulted said the human mouth is basically filthy. There's even photos of the guy afterwards, with his eye sockets plugged up and covered with some kind of skin graft and a gaping hole of yellow cartilage and scabbed blood where his nose used to be. When he was able to talk, he told police the attacker accused him of stealing his Bible, then said he was going to rape him. He said, 'You're going to be my wife, and this is going to be a lover's concerto,' which he began singing. It was a pop hit from the sixties. Starts off 'How gentle is the rain …'" You've probably heard it. It's unbelievable!"

"Man. That is unbelievable."

"Yeah. Well, I guess the moral of the story is that nothing is unbelievable. But you see what I mean? Not like your cannibal at all. German cannibalism is very rational, civilized even. There's mutual consent, good wine, precision butchery. It probably ought to be legal, just a variety of fetishism. Ours is way more crude, with the drugs and the rape and the idiotic religious angle. Typical of our two countries, don't you think? Kind of like the difference between Bach and Quentin Tarantino."

Dieter laughed. "Shit, that's funny, man. Oh, I like this song, man," he added, looking up into the air. "Doom. World of Shit. Perfect. Should be the anthem of the Earth. A big dying ball of shit."

I ordered another beer. Dieter was on his third vodka and water. He went on.

"I had a friend, German guy, went crazy over this whole thing. First, he starts to say that everything here is made out of death, the whole place, the culture, the language, the food, and then us too, the people, and all the ideas we are speaking and thinking. I remember he said Americans are made of corn and Germans are made of death. Well, he said the Americans are made of death too, but this was not his problem. Then he says he's going on a hunger strike against himself; to clean the death from his body, he's not going to eat anymore, meditating all the time to clean his mind from German; "German germs." But not just German, the whole Kapitalismus thing, patented food, slave labor, rain tax. Everything is death. But it's too late to fight it, because now it is us, he says. We're made of it. Huge eyes coming out of his head when he says this, like light bulbs. OK. He locks himself in his apartment, not talking to anybody. On the third or fourth day, he called and asked me to come by. So I go, and he gives me a big lock and asks me to close it on the door from the outside. He already put the rings to hold the lock. He has one for the inside too. He wants to shut himself inside with both locks and wants me to keep the keys. I'm thinking, OK man, I'll do it. Klaus had some crazy ideas before, and probably I'm going to come back in a week and let him out when this bullshit passes by. Let him do his thing, yeah?

"Before we closed him in, he took his cell phone and smashed it into small pieces with a hammer and then threw them in the toilet and flushed it, laughing, and said now he felt like wiping his ass, which I thought was pretty funny, and we're both laughing, and then he said, OK, goodbye, please get out, and don't forget to close the lock outside. He closed his door, and I heard him shut the lock on his side, and then he pushes the key out under the door. That's it. So now no phone, and he's locked in. I guess he can shout out the window if he wants

to get out. There's fucking stores and people on the street under his window. It's totally absurd.

"Then a week went by, and I didn't hear anything and started to worry, so I went by to his place and banged on the door,
you know, hey Klaus, man, you still alive in there? He said
yeah, what do you want? What do you mean what do I want?
I've known you twenty fucking years, you're my friend, man.
You're not finished with this shit yet? Aren't you getting hungry? He told me just go away, he doesn't want to talk, friendship is a bourgeois illusion. There's no friendship in Auschwitz.
Some shit like that, but he gave me some letter under the door,
like read that if you want to know what's going on. OK, so
I went home and tried to read the thing, and it's some typical Quatsch about how everyone must become a vegetarian
and do meditation and STOP everything, and then some stuff
about Amerika with a k and how Hitler was schwul and now
he understands what Jesus was talking about. Oh, and that
Germans will never understand Jesus because we are the white
Mongols. Immune to the Bible. The fucking Bible again,
man. Crazy people love that fucking book! When people start
talking about Hitler and Jesus together, it's not a good sign, so
I think he really needed to eat something. I go and get some
chocolate bars, went back and put them under the door. It's
an old building with space under the door. Hopefully he eats
them and comes out, yeah? I bang on the door and tell him
I put the chocolate, and he comes and pushes it back out. I
push it in again and he pushes it out, like some old black-and-
white slapstick film, in out, in out, chocolate bars sliding on

the floor. One more time and he yells take that shit away from
here. Sugar! Capitalist shit! Children slaves in Africa! Murder-
ing the Incas! It's ridiculous. I'm like, hey man, this is good
chocolate, Swiss, nice stuff, nobody killed any Incas. Great! he
screams, Swiss, the land of Jewish teeth. Go eat the Inca bones
with the gold Jewish teeth! More Nazi shit, get out, fuck off,
blah, blah, blah.

"So what should I do now? Call the cops? I hate the fucking
cops, man. Give him a few more days? I mean, now it's pretty
clear he's crazy, you know? What's going to happen? Jump out
the window, start a fire? Or maybe he's not crazy. There was
some guy in Syria fifteen hundred years ago who lived on top
of a column for thirty years and died up there, and the birds ate
him. Now he's some small kind of saint. I guess nobody called
the cops about him, or back then this was normal. Anyway, the
whole fucking thing was such a waste of time. He should have
just moved to Florida—oh, maybe not Florida but somewhere
else, somewhere warm, just get out of Germany and relax, man,
live your life. Walk on the beach, have a kid or something.
Whatever. I didn't know what to do. So I called his mother,
which is maybe worse than calling the police. But she took care
of it."

"How did it end up?"

"Ja, a few more days, and he passed out or stopped answer-
ing to anyone. His mother called the police, and they broke
the door, and he was all fucked-up. Super dehydrated. They
took him away and fed him and gave him medication, and he
became OK, but not the same guy anymore. Now he's taking

the stuff, like, twelve years, and he's a bit fat and soft, even with some small tits. And sometimes he laughs about it, but not so comfortably, like he's guilty about the medicine or the tits. But it makes you think, man. What if some Roman doctor gave some drugs to Jesus, calm him down, no need to crucify him—what kind of world would it be now if Jesus had tits?"

"Yeah, if the Romans had Prozac … that's an interesting thought. Maybe we'd be having this conversation on Mars."

"Listen, man, I really got to go now. But I am a painter, and I would like to paint your face. It's why I asked you for the matches. Maybe you could sit for me some time. And we could keep talking. Or you can come and see my work, and I would give you a couple of drawings if you sit. Maybe you will like them. My studio is very near to here, yeah? Here's my card. Give me a call if you would do this."

He handed me a black card with his name and number and a barbed-wire motif in gold, coiling along the edges of the rectangle like a delicate ivy.

IV

Where did you go, Catullus? You flashed in the pan in the first century BC and disappeared, but no one knows why or how: they just assume that you died somewhere around the year 55. I always figured if you had, we'd have heard about it; if you choked on your vomit or were stabbed by a jealous husband, at least there'd be a line or two in the surviving gossip or a letter of Cicero, but no, there's nothing. I prefer to think you just quit writing, maybe blew town and became an old beachcomber or opened a bar in some nowhere town by the sea. Outta there. Fuck that bitch, Lesbia. Fuck Rome and all the sleazy frauds that live there. I hope that's what happened, but sometimes I wish you'd stuck around a little longer and tossed off a few more poems.

The thing is, not only did you disappear, your writing almost did too. I guess it was too racy for the Christians, and they tried to get rid of it. They almost succeeded. It was gone for centuries until, in 1305, a ratty manuscript turned up in your hometown of Verona, got copied, then vanished as well. That's when we first really saw you. Purely by accident. We know almost nothing about you or about how your writing was originally organized. Somebody compiled those poems in the manuscript, but there's no way to know whether you wanted them arranged that way or if any of what you wrote is true: just that you wrote a little book, as you say in the first poem to Cornelius. But it doesn't matter, because they work the way they are—a whole story emerges from the parts like a mirage, your miserable affair with Lesbia especially, but all that other stuff as well: you hanging out with friends in Rome, drinking and writing poetry, screwing other boys and girls, like that big-nosed, short-fingered overpriced hooker with the wet mouth, or Asinius stealing your napkin, or Gellius with semen on his lips like cream, then mocking all those lisping hipsters and assholes. You move so easily from the most deli-cate refinement to the crudest obscenity, one minute crying in your beer, impotent and maudlin with love, then threatening to ram your cock up the ass and down the throats of some vulgar morons. How this guy bleached his teeth with piss, that guy stank like a goat and couldn't get laid, your wallet full of spider webs, the nose. Then your brother died—hard for you to deal.

You even insulted Julius Caesar a number of times and got his attention doing it. Before he became the godfather of Rome. I love Poem 29, where you called him *Cinaede*

Romule, "little fudge-packer Romulus … founder of Rome who takes it in the ass like a rent boy."[1] And in the same poem, mocking his rapacity and greed, you mention his *diffututa mentula*, "his fucked-out cock," exhausted from violating everyone around him. You couldn't possibly have imagined that just a few years from then, Caesar would wage and win a civil war, take over the government and become dictator, reduce his former friends to servile toadies, and a few years after that, impregnate Cleopatra, be declared dictator for life, then assassinated, turned into a comet, and made a god. Katasterized. The Divine Julius. What a load of horseshit! Or that the whole Roman thing would dissolve into more civil war and chaos and emerge as a military dictatorship in the phony guise of the republic restored. You were just insulting someone you saw as a pompous crook on the rise, with a gang of malignant cronies—the type of guy who'd put his face on a coin.

We know that Caesar heard these things and was offended, even called your father and told him to tell you to cool it.

---

[1] Cinaedus is a hard word to translate, something in the neighborhood of rent boy, butt-fucker, cocksucker, and so on. It's a term of contempt, not because of the homosexuality as such, which was no big deal, but because disgrace belonged to the penetrated. It's the passivity which was considered despicable. The word appears all over the walls of Pompeii, on the temple of Venus, or the ruins of brothels and bars, in phrases that barely need to be translated:

Albanus cinaedus est
Albanus is a cinaedus

They say he had you over for dinner. Who knows? Did that
have anything to do with why you disappeared?

But what were you supposed to do? You didn't want to
write about the big Roman themes or flatter rich patrons. I always loved that about you. You never say anything about Roman exceptionalism or the virtues of conquest. None of that
civilize-the-barbarians-white-man's-burden-type propaganda
at all. And then there was Lesbia, a married high-society girl
from the Claudii, the oldest family in Rome. You were madly
in love with her, but what did you think would happen? You
had a good time for a while. Wrote some great poems about
the fun of being with her, kissing her, how stunning, elegant
and charming she was. Did your copy of Sappho. For what? In
the end, she doesn't seem to have cared that much. She canned
you. Then started boning that pretty boy Caelius. You didn't

Secundus Carari cinaedus
Secundus is the cinaedus of Cararus
    Corneli Caesi cinaede
Hey, Cornelius Caesus, you cinaedus!

and so on. One Latin dictionary defines it as "he who practices unnatural
lust, a sodomite, catamite." Catamite is maybe as close a word as English
has to get to the truth, even though it's a bit too highbrow to capture the
flavor. It's defined by the OED as "a boy kept for homosexual purposes;
(or) the passive partner in anal intercourse." Its etymology is traced to the
Greek name Ganymede, who was a beautiful young prince from Troy,
abducted by Zeus in the form of an eagle to serve as his "cup bearer" on
Mount Olympus, meaning he served Zeus his booze and was his sex toy.
Eventually his name degenerated into a common noun, from Ganymede to
catamite, like a lexical tale of being loved and cast aside.

take it well. More poems about what a faithless cunt she was, insatiable, a slut, hanging out with drunks in shitty bars. Finally, you painted her as a common whore, blowing all comers out at the crossroads whorehouse.

I like to imagine what you'd have done with our president in America now, named Trump, believe it or not. It's a good name. He has the outsized vulgarity of those corrupt old Roman plutocrats. The bloat and venality. Likes to put his name on buildings. And we already hear things about him that sound like some of your poems, that he's a "pussy grabber," or liked to have Slavic prostitutes pee on him or lick his anus with ice cream on their tongues. You'd have had a lot of fun with him. Better than I can, anyway. I don't really know how to do it. Maybe it's the kind of thing where you need the hindsight of history, because right now, who knows what's going to happen? It does seem like the current trend is bad, that we're in for more confusion and violence—the rule of a grotesque corporate oligarchy. Maybe the pendulum will swing the other way, and these guys will just become footnotes, flunkies of a brief prominence known only to future scholars and historians. Or maybe they'll win, and the new motto of our Pax Americana will become something like it already seems to have become:

America puer merdem ede et morere

America, baby: eat shit and die.

Imagine that one, fossilized in stone or stamped into a Trump-headed three-dollar coin. Divus Donaldus. Only time will tell.

V

Well, if I were a painter, I thought, I would paint you in the glory of your nudity, your long cyclist's limbs and moonlike derriere, your elastic thorax and delicious nipples like suppliant pink macaroons. I see you on a half-shell, risen from the depths of sleep and into the surf of my awakening. There are puffy-cheeked breezes ruffling the wavelets, and grass sprouts beneath your feet as you step on the shore, copper hair pressed to your vulva in a resplendent cliché of beauty. Words flutter around you like cherubim, *oystrix, nacreous, aphrodisia*. But I am neither painter nor poet and would not insult you with these romantic idealizations. In the end, an ideal is little more than a doll, and I'd rather get back to the fact that you asked me to write you.

I was here in Berlin, walking west on Fehrbelliner Strasse. It was a cold spring morning and had rained the previous evening. There were still some thin puddles scattered around, but the sun was out, and the sky was a brilliant blue. On the pavement, at the edge of a puddle, something small and black and moving caught my eye. I bent down to investigate and found a bumblebee, wet and nearly frozen, writhing slowly on the ground like a fallen athlete. It seemed to cost him everything he had just to accomplish this movement. His wings were soaked and useless, and the sodden hairs of his fuzz were tamped down against his wet black sides. A bright orange band ringed his abdomen. He must have gotten caught and downed in the rain, like a hapless Icarus, and spent the night exposed in the bitter cold. I considered crushing him to put him out of his misery: a quick pop of his thoracic capsule and the pain would be reduced to a smear of inert gelatin. It was about 9:30 in the morning. Right nearby was a metal cabinet about shoulder height, the top of which was blazing yellow in the sunlight, so I picked him up and set him on the warm surface to see if would help him to revive. Immediately he began to squirm and stretch his limbs. I could almost feel the heat seeping through and warming into his core. I leaned in close and exhaled onto him, and the moist heat of my breath added to the sunlight seemed to bathe and ooze through him like an orgasm. He began expanding his segments and rolling from side to side, stroking and brushing himself with his forelegs. After five or six long, slow breaths and the time spent drying in the sun, his wings suddenly exploded into motion, buzzing and blurring the light around them to a shimmering golden halo. I began vibrating my vocal cords as I breathed over him, and even though his eyes were the same expressionless black light bulbs, it felt like we were communicating in a strange way, him buzzing and expanding and me moaning over him and exhaling into his prickly little hairs. A few more breaths and he was gone, up and off, in a wide, curving trajectory. Beautiful.

This morning I woke up and thought of that half-frozen bee. I was stiff and sore and cold. The windows had been open all night in the bedroom, and the wind was shrieking and rattling the panes. The cross-ventilation was fierce, and the temperature must have been close to zero. I know you like to sleep naked in the freezing air, bundled under layers of blanket and down, but my limbs were beaten down and stiff, and the night was still black outside. I felt old and immobile, grappling with demons of failure, and the universe seemed empty and malicious. Well, get up and close the window, you might have said, and soon the dawn will appear, but you were far away in New York, and I was huddled and shivering here in Berlin. What I really missed was my lithe red angel, to appear from above, or below or beyond, to warm me and light me and blow me back to humanity.

VI

My apartment in Berlin had one of those old-fashioned toilets with a strange design feature they call the "shit-shelf." It's a German thing, meaning the bowl is not the simple, open, half-full funnel of water we have in America, where you flush and everything is sucked down away through the bottom. Instead, this toilet has a horizontal ledge at the back that lies directly under you when you sit, and a smaller, well-like vertical waste shaft at the front. So when you go, the turd extrudes itself onto this shelf and sits there underneath you, on display. And this is the explanation I've been given: the shelf is for inspection, and you should inspect your excrement—its color, smell, consistency, etc.—for clues to the state of your health. It's a strange thought. Did Germans keep a set of peculiar utensils, I wondered, some kind of home proctology kit, with rubber gloves and a microscope? Glass slides and a cheese knife? As an American, I felt a bit backward. Provincial and disgusted. You can feel the mound sitting there under you; the heat is palpable, and, because it's out in the air and not submerged in water, the smell is much more powerful, sometimes even eye-watering. To be honest, I'd rather have had a different bathroom, but it also seemed absurd to avoid my own toilet bowl. Know thyself, as it were, I figured: no?

I'd never been that interested in my own feces before, but the condition of using this toilet made it somehow inevitable. And my bowels seemed to respond. I began to eliminate these monstrous turds, black and coiling like snakes, sometimes seeming like they must have weighed five or six pounds. Where the hell did they come from? I could feel the difference in my body weight when done, and I'd get up feeling much lighter, as if relieved of decay. Then I felt compelled to inspect, with a strange mixture of fascination and disgust that something so vivid and repulsive had come out of me. It was almost like a regression to toilet training. I couldn't help thinking of Freud and his psychosexual phases of development, oral, anal, phallic, and so on; in this case, obviously, the anal phase, between the ages of eighteen months and three years old, when you gain control of the anal sphincter; supposedly then your attention and libidinal energies gravitate there and away from the oral sphincter. Or, as the German puts it, from the Mundschleimhaut to the Darm-und-Urogenitalschleimhaut, that is, from the oral mucosa to the bowel-and-urogenital mucosa. I love that German word for mucosa, *Schleimhaut*, which literally means "slimeskin." Anyway, phase two, the anal. Time for toilet training. The first demands of civilization in the social-ized control of excretion. The party's over, kid. You can't just piss and shit as you please anymore. Time to become a citizen of the world. However, with the correct training and positive reinforcement, you learn that feces can be a gift and that its proper handling is the essence of a well-ordered society. Funda-mental, you might say. Then you're ready to move on. At least, that's the idea. But things can go wrong. As we all know, you can get stuck or "fixated" in the anal phase. If your toilet-train-ers are too strict or tyrannical, you may become frightened and hesitant, holding it in for fear of punishment. Maybe it's not the right time? For the rest of your life, you'll be scarred by this as an "anal retentive," compulsively neat, cheap, submissive to authority, puritanical; everyone knows the type. On the other hand, if they're too lax, you may become an "anal expulsive," careless, sloppy, prodigal, rebellious, a tasteless hedonist.

I don't really remember how my own training went, but I'd have to deduce that my parents were a bit too relaxed, be-cause I've definitely turned out as an expulsive. I'm unkempt and thoughtless. My life is a mess. I can't seem to hold on to money, and I hate being told what to do. Even my name is an anagram of *anal*, as if it were written into my destiny. In a way this whole book is kind of an anal expulsion, without much structure or purpose, just trying to entertain with some of a life's digested residues. A necessary self-indulgence masquerad-ing as a gift. The title itself is just an extension of the anagram: *Animal* is *I'm Alan*.

VII

Or think of Augustine, another expulsive—moaning and pontificating to God with such masochistic theatricality, so intimate and public at the same time, like a kind of religious masturbation. *The Confessions* is such a strange performance of a book; one minute it seems to make perfect sense, and another it doesn't, like God is The Hologram, now you see it, now you don't: is IT there, or isn't it? Like everyone, sometimes I find myself talking to God, too, with a weird inner certainty that my words are being listened to and that there must be a divine witness and cause for all of this, this mystery of consciousness, and the infinite inner depth we have: how couldn't there? So simple. I'll say thanks for the blessing, Boss, or how could you do that, or who am I and how could I do that, between the usual bouts of shame and exaltation. But I don't feel like I'm alone. I was made for a purpose, and the world seems to have meaning. And then I'll catch myself, like when a stranger sees you doing something ridiculous, picking your nose or scratching your ass in public, and I'll laugh in embarrassment. Come on, Alan, I'll say. Who do you think you're talking to? You and I both know there's nothing out there. There's this and nothing more. You're a walking pillar of ashes. Remember your Roman tombstones. And everyone knows this feeling in some form or other, even if they despise or reject it. We all know it because we grew up with it. I call it the Judeo-Christian funeral mask: you put it on and remember the minds of the ancestors. Thou shalt not this. Thou shalt not that. The Lord is a jealous god. I don't know about you, but to me the biblical religion stuff doesn't make much sense anymore. I don't believe Moses received the Law from God or that Jesus transubstantiated and resurrected, or that Allah spoke to Mohammed. I can imagine saying I believe these things if I were going to be killed or tortured for refusing, and I can see why authorities would have an interest in enforcing all the prohibitions and compulsions that go along with such ideas, but now that we're almost free to ignore them, they seem obsolete already, like ideological fossils.

VIII

I was in Paris recently and went into the vast gothic Cathedral of Notre Dame. It's the real deal, with cavernous vaulting full of stained glass and teeming with gloomy sculptures of gargoyles and saints and damnation. Sound echoes and rises up through the dark blue light like dissipating prayer—it really creates a feeling of the sublime. And it's busy, full of tourists milling around, people praying at the various chapels, homeless men sitting on folding chairs and reading newspapers over the heating grates in the floor. Outside there are lines to get in and paramilitary-style police with black berets and machine guns protecting everything from terrorism. But it made me wonder: What does a cathedral like this become when the God to which it was dedicated is obsolete? Is it like a pagan temple of antiquity, a ruin or a tourist site, or an object of art history? Or more like the skeleton of a dinosaur, no longer alive but still with an immense grandeur and dignity? Or does it become retrospectively grotesque, like a fascist monument, or a Mt. Rushmore, pointing to a time of totalitarian monotheism? I found it hard to see. During the French Revolution, the cathedral was vandalized, desecrated, and reconsecrated as a temple to freedom, with a statue of liberty replacing the virgin who was locked away in the basement. Then, for a while, it was used as a warehouse before becoming restored. And what about the relics: the crown of thorns, the true cross, and the holy nail? Are they fraudulent? Quaint? Ridiculous? Like the twelve foreskins of Jesus scattered around the churches of Europe? Leo Allatius, a seventeenth-century Greek scholar and theologian, vampire expert, and custodian of the Vatican Library, argued in an unpublished work, *De Praeputio Domini Nostri Jesu Christi Diatriba*, that the foreskin of Christ could not have remained on Earth after the Ascension but must also have transcended, and not only that: rather than reattaching itself to the transubstantiated glans, it went out into the heavens and became the rings of Saturn. Isn't that fantastic? Obviously not a mainstream idea, but not really any less plausible than the parting of the Red Sea, or the resurrection, or retroactively baptizing the souls of the Holocaust dead in a giant toilet bowl in Utah. I guess it depends who you ask. The unshaved clochard at his paper, the polyglot tourists, or that gaunt old lady on her knees in the corner, quietly mumbling her rosaries ...

IX

Dieter's place was a cavernous old loft in Kreuzberg, just a few blocks from the bar where I'd met him. It was like something from an old black-and-white documentary about New York painters in the fifties. Fifteen-foot ceilings with huge windows, peeling white walls, and wide, paint-spattered floorboards, warped and uneven, with gaping cracks between them. Bathtub in the kitchen. Furniture culled from the streets and flea markets, doors and slabs of wood propped up on concrete bricks as tables. His studio was half the space, in the back by the windows, and he'd set an armchair of threadbare green velour at an angle against the wall so the daylight would hit me as I sat there. The sun bounced into the loft off a large blank wall from the building next door.

We didn't talk much at first. He motioned me over to the chair with a preoccupied nod. I sat down, and he sat opposite me on a stool and immediately began sketching onto a canvas with a small stump of charcoal.

After about twenty minutes, he said, "You got a cool face, man. A bit beat up, you know, like dented somehow. I like the nose especially—you broke it, no?"

"Oh, a couple of times—only once badly though. But you're right. The bone is dented. My skull is like a dented can."

"Looks like a fighter's nose. Were you ever boxing?"

"No. Motorcycle accident. Messed up my arm and neck too. You know the American cartoon character Popeye?"

"Ja, man. The sailor who eats the spinach and punches the fat guy for the skinny girl? I liked this one."

"Remember how his arm looked when he ate the spinach? Check this out."

I pulled up my sleeve and bent my left arm to flex the bicep. The torn muscle curled up and bulged grotesquely under the skin like a ping-pong ball. Dieter laughed.

"Popeye. Ha ha. That's pretty good, man. You didn't have a helmet to cover your face? You like to play with your life?"

"I guess I was a bit self-destructive back then, but that was a long time ago. I didn't really care if I lived or died. Not anymore. But I've definitely used up some lives. You say that in German?"

"Ja. Die neun Leben der Katze."

Some time went by in silence.

"What do you do here in Berlin?"

"I was working on a book, but I'm not sure if that's true anymore. My motivation seems to be dissolving."

"And about what is your book?"

"I don't know. It was going to be a broken-hearted love story, a crazy love affair that ends for no reason. The girl disappears. The guy goes off the deep-end, tears himself up, analyzes and harps over everything, a little history of ancient literature, a murder, some cheap sex and boozing. Partially based on something that happened to me that really fucked me up, but it's been a few years, and I guess I don't really care anymore. I got bored of writing about it. Girl got married, had a kid, the scab turned into a scar. It doesn't hurt anymore. So why should anyone else care? It's the oldest cliché in the book. Who needs another one? But I'm still working on it. I'll probably put this conversation in it, even though at this point you're still a semi-fictional character. I'm not sure I can use you yet."

"Who you calling semi-fictional, man? Fuck you." He laughed. "Maybe I'm doing the same thing to you. Mimetic Exploitismus. But it doesn't matter if you don't know what you're doing. Just keep working. What else can you do? And those stories are good. Everybody has one. It's why you do it, right? Doesn't matter if it's a cliché. It's better if it's a cliché. At least you're talking about something people understand. Not some bullshit. Like a naked woman. How many fucking naked woman paintings there are? It's not a cliché?"

X

I wanted to write something like Catullus, about a love that filled my head with beautiful illusions for a minute, then ended and left me feeling miserable and impotent for a long time. That is something right in his line, like his poems about Lesbia. And I want to do it like he did, straightforward, in direct address, just tell the story, warts and everything. Like Cato intoned, through rustic beard:

rem tene verba sequentur

have something to say, the words will follow.

And in a way, this book is an homage to Catullus, though I should probably explain a little more: it's not a novel and not intended to be one. I'm not sure what it is, anymore than I know what Catullus's work amounts to as a whole in formal terms. The continuities are thematic rather than narrative. It's a smattering of clusters and shards, some better or more interesting than others, long, short, petty, deep, precious, obscene, lyric, elegiac, hexametrical. A little something for everyone. You take what you need and move on. Anyway, it never bothered me, and I hope that my attempts to be similar won't bother you. I hope that you're having a good time and won't get bored or walk away.

XI

It's been a minute, as they say, Lucita. At least a couple of years. I'm in Berlin again, in an apartment this time, not that garret room I was in when you visited, with the beams and the vaulted ceiling with its skewed triangular rafters. It's pretty bare. I have a bed, a table, and a life-sized anatomical model of a skeleton standing propped in the corner. He's missing a few teeth, and his left foot dangles awkwardly, with the toes pointing backward as if from a badly broken ankle. In his jaws there's a sprig of dried lavender, and next to him a stem of dead purple lilies in a wine bottle. The petals are shriveled and curled like molted snakeskins, but they still haven't dropped. It's like a gloomy still life or a poem from Horace: the skeleton, the empty wine bottle, the lavender, an empty white wall. I even named the skeleton M&M for memento mori. Sometimes I just call him Maury, like an old Jewish uncle.

Remember Thomas? He still asks about you. He's as melancholy and beautiful as ever; his sad blue eyes still the same, only now they're deep behind a large, dense beard with a lot of gray in it. His voice is still that soft, melodious murmur. It's great to see him again. He even built me the table at which I'm writing this. It's straight and high, sanded smooth but unvarnished—just like him. I'm a little worried about him though. He's smoking and drinking a lot, not eating much. Too skinny. Apart from the booze and nicotine, he seems to be getting little pleasure out of life these days. It's like there's something implacable inside him, an anger at vulgarity or an inability to act in his own interest that I sometimes think is driving him quietly insane. I don't think he knows what to do with himself. (I guess that makes two of us.) Other times I think maybe he doesn't want anything at all, which is a simultaneously beautiful and difficult problem to have. I don't know. He doesn't say much, so it's hard to tell. One day he seems almost saintly, another almost clinically depressed. Whatever it is, it gives him an air of deep and gentle loneliness, something very far away. In another age he might have been a mystic, living in a mountain cave somewhere and hanging out with the birds. But then there's his sense of humor, scathing, quipped in barbs that flash like an unsheathed blade. I don't know if you knew this, but he was once a competitive fencer. He'll lean back, shaking with laughter and raising the front legs of his chair, then drop back down again, slamming the chair legs onto the floor and coughing into his hands. The smoker's hack is bad right now; you can hear the mucus shuffling around in his lungs.

He's forty-six I think, no children, never been married: in some ways we're very similar. When we look at each other and drink beer in silence, I'm struck by that question: What are you supposed to do in this life if you don't have children? We're breeding machines, like any other plant or animal, geared to survive, to compete and multiply. It seems so obvious: you have children, you have something to do, an ingrained purpose and set of behaviors. Love, feed, protect, it's life, it's natural, and not to do so is unnatural, a rejection somehow, a judgment against. Or perhaps it's a kind of psychosomatic sterility, a result of all the psychic and physical pollution around us. A fish in a dirty stream experiencing its own poisoning as depression and inability to spawn. Why bother?

Before I met you, I never wanted a child. I was actually against it, for the usual reasons. The world was too crowded and brutal. People were horrible, myself included. You go numb just from reading the news. I was too old, burnt out. The earth wouldn't last much longer anyway. No more oil, no more water, no more oxygen, no more elephants or rhinos or bees. No meaningful tomorrow. Soon it would be a nightmare of zombie cannibals trolling a landscape of scorched machinery and corpses. Who would bring a child into such a world? Besides, I didn't really like the life of people I knew with children: the constant exhaustion, the pressure and fear, their own infantilization and slavery, the goo-goo talk, the fetishism, the screaming, the shit-filled diapers. That life seemed like drudgery. It didn't appeal to me. I just wanted to be free. Besides, it was better people like me be bred out of the population. The species didn't need defective specimens. I'd probably end up a sad and seedy old man shuffling around the train station in a piss-stained raincoat.

Then there was our summer together and that last night before you left for China, and I didn't want you to go, but how could I tell you to stay? I knew your restlessness, your craving to roam free, and I loved that about you. (I was the same way.) That was your plan before we got together, and you told me so, so fair is fair. You stuck to your plan. But still it made me sad that you wanted to go more than you wanted me. Simple enough. I should have understood that better then. I should have seen that writing on the wall. That last night, I was overcome by a desire to make you pregnant. I hadn't seen that coming at all: it exploded on me. Was I trying to keep you by tying you down with a child? Or was it simple animal love, a pheromone or some mysterious confluence of testosterone and dopamine finally throwing the breeding switch in my nature? How does one ever know these things? You're probably not supposed to ask the question, but even that "supposed" implies some teleology: supposed by whom? Anyway, I tried. We made love so hard I thought we might hurt each other. I imagined my seed flowing into you like magma, saw it glowing over and wrapping your ovules. I felt sure you would become pregnant. And you knew what I was thinking, though neither of us said anything. When we lay back next to each other in that pant-and-stare-at-the-ceiling afterglow, I was dazed at the emotion blowing through the room, like a wind coming into the window, as if you were a tree and I were your rustling leaves or we weren't even there at all. Just life, pure and impersonal. I put my head on your chest and listened to the thud of your heartbeat and thought "this." This was what I was waiting for without even knowing. It's a paradox: you made me believe in the soul by turning me into an animal. The next day you left, on a train to California and from there for your slow boat to China. I watched your train pull out and your face disappear, and didn't know if I would ever see you again.

Well, you didn't get pregnant. We went our separate ways. It didn't seem like you were coming back from China. It was just going to be a beautiful memory. I was probably too old for you anyway, fourteen years, etc., etc. We faded away from each other through a lengthening tunnel of fewer and fewer emails. Happy Birthday. Happy New Year. I met somebody, you met somebody, blah dee blah, blah, blah. A year went by, ten or twelve time zones away.

And then your sister was murdered. Shot in the face in her own kitchen. You were in Russia visiting a friend, and you called me in Berlin immediately. I remember I was sitting in my friend Colin's office when the phone rang, some unknown number. I almost didn't answer it, but when I did, it was you, your voice a breathless rattle, and you told me. I'll never forget how you sounded in that moment, so lost and inconsolable. Like you were quietly, barely screaming. I'm hot, you said, my body is hot like a fever. I don't know anything. Croaking and quavering. Alan, you said. Alan. I don't want to churn that up here or to disrespect your family, but I need to express what happened in me when you told me, so much pain and disgust and rage—I wanted to smash everything in the room. To beat the shit out of Colin, who was sitting there watching me with raised eyebrows, not knowing what was going on but knowing it was something terrible. But it was strange, because I knew that emotion wasn't mine—it was yours, channeling into me through the phone. I loved your sister too, but it wasn't like any pain I'd felt over the death of anyone close to me. Not even my father's. And that made me believe in something I didn't understand before, which was selfless, empathetic love: I felt you were me. You were my other half. I had absorbed the Platonic cliché. And I wanted to vomit. I wanted that pain to wash over me, soak me like a hot, disgusting wave, if it could just help you, if I could relieve you of some of it by feeling it myself. I was proud of the purity of that emotion. It made me love you even more. And I think it was at that point that I began to lose touch with reality, to idealize you, as a victim of tragedy and a soul in sorrow that it was my job to heal and defend, a beautiful instinct that festered into a delusion. Because I couldn't do that, and you were alone, thousands of miles away.

And then, two years later, you came back to me, to Berlin, for a week, and we went on, picked up right where we left off, New York for a few days, New Hampshire, Vermont, you moved to Hawaii, we met in Las Vegas, all the places we saw each other for a few days at a time, a few days of inhumanly beautiful sex and love, but never longer, never long enough to get normal or boring. For months we were apart, me in Vermont and you in Hawaii, writing letters, poems, texts, Skyping, in a constant state of desire and frustration.

It became morbid. I thought about you all the time, convinced myself you were with me and that I was experiencing that exaltation in love that Plato described, winged souls hovering between worlds, aloft in telepathy. I believed those things, senseless as it might seem now. And you sent me such beautiful letters, poems, sprigs from your garden, locks of your hair. I found one recently, folded inside that entomology textbook I gave you while you were grieving in the cabin in New Hampshire. I opened it to look up something and the letter fell out, a folded piece of pale-yellow notebook paper torn from a spiral. A little bundle of dry blond hair bound in red thread. Your neat little scrawl in black felt-tip pen. You were teasing me for my love of dictionary definitions and wrote:

To Morrow: to know and accept one's soul mate while denying the existence of such things.

So I do accept this passion and that it is solefully, soulfully directed at you as part of my foundation ... Ours is the most ethical expense of energy. The beautiful stew of past knuckles, knees, blood, semen, a scrambled universe of slippery roads and soft landings. To morrow with you is easy. Because I love you and my spirit is awake.

I was in Vermont when you wrote that, convinced we would be together as soon as my job was over. But I must not have known who you were anymore, or at least what you were thinking, because it came as a complete shock when you ended it. Just a month or two later. Out of the blue. The you you had become to me wouldn't have done that. How could she? First you switched off the telepathy. I felt it the moment it happened, just like that; the line went dead. Then a few weeks later I was in New York, anxiously waiting for you to arrive in a few days, when you texted me. Was I free for lunch tomorrow? LUNCH? I thought. You're already here? Are you fucking serious?

So that's what I'm left with, wondering what happened or what it ever was. How all those words crumbled into a heap of meaningless gravel. Did I make it all up? Or was it like Catullus says: What a woman says to her craving lover should be written in water and wind? Or did you need me to get yourself through the pain of losing your sister and then not anymore? Had I become a reminder of her murder? Or did I offend you in some way I couldn't see? Was it my drinking, my obscenity, my servile adoration? Or maybe it just stopped. You woke up and it was gone, evaporated, head and heart clear. And I'm haunted by my own hypocrisy, the thought that all I wanted from you was your beauty, to consume you sexually, that I was fantasizing and would have grown bored, that I was in a mating rut, which would have worn off into an eternity of balding tedium. I know I wouldn't have wanted to see your perfect little ass pulled apart from child bearing or your virginal breasts collapsed into bags from nursing. An ugly idea, I know, but that doesn't make it any less true. Maybe I would have grown beyond it, but I'll never know. You weren't here to bring out that dubious best in me.

PS: Since I wrote the first draft of this book, I heard you had a child. Joe from the bar told me; she saw it on Facebook. So I went and looked and found the picture: you and your husband holding a blank-looking, red-headed baby. It's a strange picture, the three of you in an empty apartment or maybe a house, like a stock photo almost or a real-estate ad: lovely young family. You can't tell if the child is a boy or a girl or where this young family is, but it doesn't look like Hawaii. Something about the wood flooring and the hinges on the closet doors, the heating vent in the floor, and your clothing. Your husband has on a wool hat and sweater. The baby has a sweater too, and you're wearing dark jeans and black leather ankle boots. Did you go back east to New Hampshire and buy a house? I wish I could ask you those questions and not be that pathetic guy peeping into the window on Facebook, or that I could call you on the phone and ask you, how are you doing? Are you happy? Do you ever regret leaving me? I don't really know what I feel. Pain, that that baby should be ours? Or relief at escaping domesticity? Or both? But I can't call that you anymore. That you is gone, and so is the me that knew her. Ghosted. Like that Roman epitaph: I was not, I was, I'm not. Who cares? The bridge is gone, dissolved into water and wind.

XII

But I still think about you often. Some time ago I was riding my bike on a cloudy day through some backwoods roads in Vermont, flying the curves, the beginnings of autumn bursting out in small red patches on the still-luxuriant green. All that space and light and green. It was heaven. I thought I understood what Socrates meant in the *Phaedo*, the day he died, the day he drank the poison so cheerfully, about the body being a prison that the soul wants to escape. There's a pun involved: *soma* in Greek means body, and *sema* means sign and also tombstone, so the idea is that the body is a tomb-like prison, a somatic, semantic incarnation, and what we think of as life is actually more like death, an idea basic to both Platonism and Christianity. That there's somewhere else to go, some amalgam of mind and outer space as paradise.

I wasn't really feeling that, but just a kind of impatience or claustrophobia about my own being, about this, this form of life we are, with arms and legs and a mind and genitals. I was tired of being miserable about you and knowing that it came mostly from my body, like an addiction withdrawal. I wanted something else, something I can't put my finger on, but obviously something "higher," whatever that might mean. I didn't want to be a man or a woman or anything that has to eat and shit and fuck and die. I guess that doesn't leave much to imagine. I don't know. Something else. A different set of needs and possibilities. A deep, old spiritual fantasy with the usual imprecise metaphors. Like what does a plant or insect feel as it grasps and veers toward the light? Maybe it's as simple as that and just as mechanical, a phototropism of the gelatin in my skull.

I know it sounds ridiculous, but I didn't want to feel degraded by my need for pleasure anymore. By my addictions and cravings. The tyranny of my penis. It still stuns me how such a trivial thing—the need to get it rubbed and squirt its sperm can be so domineering. It's like there's two of you, or it's like having a dog, with its own needs and impulses; he has to be fed and walked, you get home from work and he's jumping up and down and panting, and if you ignore him, eventually he'll piss and shit on the floor. Leave him too long and he'll start howling and destroying things, bite you or drive you insane. You have to rub him and scratch him and pick up his turds in a bag, like a sodden condom—the proof of his life: a plastic bag full of hot organic material.

And I know it's absurd and obvious to say, but I wouldn't

have loved you so obsessively if I didn't have that thing. Maybe not even at all, and that bothers me. As if it wasn't me at all, or you, but pheromones and breeding mechanisms, rut and heat, whipping us around like puppet fools, and those emotions just part of the whirl.

I guess that's why we invent stories like the immaculate conception, of Zeus in the form of a bull or a swan or an eagle or a golden shower, visiting human women and breeding demigods. If Mary had simply gotten fucked and pregnant like any other woman, it would have diluted the symbolism of transcendence. We have to ennoble the animal, put lipstick on the pig. You were half my soul, my heart, et cetera. We weren't just two slabs of meat grubbing around at a hole. When you left me, I didn't feel like living anymore. I felt like such an idiot, like a sucker tourist who loses all his money in a shell game because he didn't know it was fixed to begin with. Standing on the corner with his dick in his hand and tears rolling down his cheeks. You were just supposed to reproduce, you moron. That platonic shit is for artists and pederasts. Now go home, back to Podunk where you belong.

But like I said, in everything there's always the script, or a role which the moment presents you to play. You can surrender yourself to play it or not. I secretly enjoyed the tragedy of abandonment you played me. You created textbook conditions for the spurned lover-poet, locked out and grieving, spinning his pain into self-indulgent lines. I think Catullus enjoyed it too, but it was also at that point that he got ugly and started talking about Lesbia fucking 300 guys or blowing people in alleyways.

He never got graphic about her when times were good. He comes off as a bit of a crybaby, then as a crybaby getting nasty, kicking and screaming. Just because you dumped me doesn't mean you're a whore. So I don't want to talk about coming down your throat or sticking my tongue up your ass, even though I loved doing those things and don't think of them as dirty. It's a matter of genre. I don't want to reduce our love to the vulgar comedy of porn. What's the point? You have to get on with your own life anyway, right, Alan?

XIII

But you know how it is when you get dumped. I fell into one of those clichéd spirals: the drinking, the drugs, the miserable promiscuity. The script—the role of the unrequited lover—all there was was to settle in and play it. It's a satisfying melodrama, because the pain seems so meaningful and the possibility of its solution so obvious. If only she'd come back to me, if only, if only: it's infantile in its simplicity, like a baby screaming for the warm oblivion of mamma.

It was a bipolar binge. Either I stayed home alone nodding out in a warm miasma of opioids, or I went out and ran around all night drinking whiskey and snorting cocaine. For a while, I was going to this after-hours club called Body Heat, which was essentially a cocaine speakeasy in the East Village. It was hidden in the parlor floor of an old house, but so insulated and blacked out you had no inkling of what was going on from outside. On the street it seemed like a dark, quiet house, even a bit funereal. A stone staircase led up one flight to a heavy, solid door. By the door, painted over and almost invisible, a discreet black doorbell. When you pushed it, a little hatch slid open and a scowling doorman gave you the once-over. The door would open, and you'd walk into a cloaked-off foyer, get patted down by a pair of enormous security goons and go through another door into a smoky, dimly lit parlor with music blasting from a boom-box in the kitchen. It was like a house party, but with waitress service and small tables and chairs scattered around. You'd sit, and the waitress would bring you, unasked, a tall-boy can of Budweiser, a small piece of cut straw, and a mini Ziploc bag of cheap cocaine, twenty dollars. I called it the Avenue C Happy Meal. The straw was a nice touch, no fumbling around rolling up money into messy tubes, and no incentive to keep that last twenty-dollar bill.

Anyway, I remember it and I don't remember it, the clusters of people doing lines together, the murky bilge of cigarette smoke in the bluish light, the frantic coke conversation of so many strangers all crazed and chattering like rattling mechanical skulls. But I don't remember anyone in particular anymore—it's like that whole time is gone, literally wasted. One night I was a little worse than usual. I probably already had a bottle of whiskey in me before I got there, and I was out of my mind on some low, long couch against the wall, smoking a cigarette and taking in the scene, thinking she wouldn't want me here, if she only knew about the purity and nobility of my suffering, she would rush back to me, take me into her arms.

She would cry and tell me what a loveless desolation her life had become since she dumped me. Or something like that, back into the script, reading my lines, wallowing in maudlin ineptitude. Then snort another line. Utres inflati ambulamus, like it says in Petronius, we're nothing but walking balloons.

A light-skinned Black guy with dyed blond hair slid himself down on the couch next to me, leaned forward with his shoulder, and spoke to me in a deep but feminine voice.

"I think you're beautiful," he said.

It was a strange moment for me. Everything falling apart. Drunk, high, drowning in loneliness and self-pity, a worthless piece of shit, I thought, but hard and laughing. That was me. I don't remember what I said. Or what he said afterward. But I remember his name was Michael. Sitting on that couch for a while and talking, drinking and snorting lines. Or at least I was. The next thing I remember was sitting on the curb at Houston Street and Avenue C in the cold dawn air kissing sloppily, clasping each other's heads, all lips and tongues and slobbering saliva. I remember being surprised and turned on and surprised at being turned on and thinking fuck that bitch anyway. Why not try something else? It's not like the straight thing is working out so well.

I took him home to my place, or maybe he just wanted to make sure I got home, which I somehow did, and we ended up in my bed, and I passed out. Or this is how I piece it together, because I woke up a few hours later, confused and badly hungover, to the feeling of being blown. At first I didn't even realize I was home or remember much of anything. I had a throbbing head, eyelids glued together, a tongue like a chunk of roadkill. Then I noticed a warm, wet sensation on my penis. I looked down, and there, crouched around my groin, with my underwear stretched out at my knees, was a blond head bobbing up and down atop a pair of broad, muscular shoulders. Wait a minute, I thought. What? Who's this guy sucking my dick? What is a man doing sucking my dick? Then it came flooding back to me: the club, the whiskey, the coke, Michael approaching me on the couch, my sudden inspiration to try being with a man, making out on Houston Street, now here I was. So what? I thought. Does it really matter? A mouth is a mouth, right? Who says no to a blowjob? But I guess I wasn't as open-minded as I thought. I couldn't get into it. My semi hard-on dwindled down to a flaccid knob he was diddling around in his mouth like a wine cork. It was embarrassing. Michael looked up in disappointment.

"Sorry, man," I said. "This just isn't working for me. I think I got a little carried away last night. Looks like no dice."

I slithered back and pulled my shorts up.

"You were pretty fucked up," he said in his strangely girly baritone. "But don't give up now. Let me keep trying …"

I thought about it for a second, but my gut said no.

"Nah. I can't do it. Sorry, but it's not my thing. Let's get out of this with no harm done, okay? We don't even know each other."

He turned and lay on his back next to me, then looked up at the ceiling and sighed. "I had such hopes for you. You're a great conversationalist. A lot like someone I really used to love."

I laughed, a little awkwardly. "I know the feeling, but I don't know what to say. I guess I'm a bit of a train wreck right now. You want a coffee? I could really use a coffee."

I got out of bed, found my jeans on the floor and pulled them on, then went over to the stovetop and started unscrewing the coffee maker, still barefoot and shirtless.

"No. No thanks," he said. "I think I'll just get out of here and go home. Try to salvage a little dignity from what's left of my Sunday. You do look cute making coffee though."

He smiled a little sadly and started putting on his clothes. A few minutes later he was out the door, and I never saw him again.

XIV

My father was a surgeon, and he told me that as medical students he and his friends started smoking heavily because it killed the smell of corpses and formaldehyde in the dissecting rooms. They spent a lot of time there studying anatomy, and the formaldehyde-cured corpses had a sickly sweet smell that was nauseating. Plus all that death. So they smoked constantly and developed some irreverent rituals to take their minds off what they were doing. For example, before starting a dissection, they would "anesthetize the patient" by hitting him or her on the head with a wooden mallet. Or a thigh bone. Sometimes they flung scalpels into a body like darts to see who could make them stick most consistently or hit a bullseye on the nipple. Beer for the winner. Once a guy put a carnation into the anus of a corpse as it lay prone and they were dismantling its spinal column. Some sort of pun about flesh and "incarnation." (British humor.) And as they smoked and worked, they would use the cadaver's mouth as an ashtray. That image has always stuck in my mind: a gutted, dried-out body with its organs on display and a gaping, brainless skull with a mouth full of cigarette butts. It seems like a perfect emblem of something, even if I don't know what it is: our brute materialism, the cynicism of the age, memento mori, something like that, condensed into a kernel of grotesque tragicomedy. When I tell people that story, they usually wince in disgust, then laugh, but they're uncomfortable with the idea of a corpse as an object of ridicule. As if it exposed a deep vulnerability, something usually concealed behind a veil of sacrament and ritual. Or with the idea of the self as a thing. You might think, shit, is that all there is? What's going to happen to my body after I die? And does it really matter whether it's worms or flames or medical students? Maybe it's really that question of whether it matters that matters, of matter mattering, of sacred and profane. Something you can't shine a light on or look at directly. And strangely, the original meaning of matter as a verb is "to secrete or discharge pus; to suppurate."

So to say that matter matters is not necessarily a tautology. It's like you end up going around in metaphorical, etymological circles. The proverbial dog chasing his pronominal tail.

XV

I was riding a bicycle through Tiergarten and saw two guys dressed in black denim about twenty meters apart kicking a soccer ball back and forth, both holding beers and smoking cigarettes. That's what you call a Berlin fitness program.

XVI

I like to bite my girlfriend's ass in the morning. She's lying on her stomach still asleep, and I clasp a piece of her right buttock in my teeth, pull it gently toward me, and nuzzle my nose into the musky intergluteal groove. I smell her smell, which is simultaneously filthy and clean, like a truffle dog rooting around in the moss of a million years. It's a rank and heavenly fuzz. Then she'll wake up and complain, "Don't smell my butt!" She'll push my head away, but she's smiling, eyes still closed. It's a very good way to start the day.

XVII

Out of the blue I was asked to write a piece about strength for *Men's Health* magazine. I don't know how they knew who I was or why they wanted me, and they never published it, but the topic made me think about when I lived in the East Village, just across from Tompkins Square Park, and I would often see a chopped old Triumph Bonneville parked around the neighborhood. It was a brushed gunmetal gray, a lean and spidery bobber, and it always made me stop and stare in envy. One day I was walking down Avenue A by Ray's Candy Store, an old, narrow soda-fountain place with a steel hotdog rotisserie and worn-out Formica countertops, the walls festooned with faded, once-garish pictures of ice-cream sundaes and old, yellowing newspaper clippings about Ray. The bike was parked outside, and I went in. There was only one other customer, in heavy jeans with a belt-loop chain, black engineer boots and a sleeveless white T-shirt, definitely the bike's owner. He was one of the biggest guys I've ever seen, not especially tall, maybe six, six one, but about three feet wide and a solid wall of muscle. The veins squirmed in his biceps like green worms, and his head and face were blunt and angular. He had silver hair shaved down to stubble on both face and scalp, and pale blue-gray eyes. A menacing, enormous presence. He was staring into space and chewing, holding the severed half of a hotdog in front of him, pointed at his face like a gun.

"Nice bike," I said.

He looked at me and swallowed the mouthful of hotdog bolus. I saw his esophagus bulge and contract around it as it slid down.

"Thanks," he grunted, then pushed the remaining hotdog half into his mouth. His jaw was the size of a cow's. I heard the sausage membrane pop as he bit down and resumed chewing, then turned away. I ordered an egg cream from the girl behind the counter.

He finished the dog and spoke.

"You know what I like about that bike?" he asked, somewhat rhetorically. His voice was surprisingly high, with a Brooklyn accent.

"What's that?" I asked.

"I can pick it up and carry it upstairs to my apartment, so I don't have to leave it on the street at night. People around here are animals."

He was looking straight into my eyes with an almost psychopathic intensity, and I had no idea if he was serious or just playing some deadpan gag. He was just big enough and the bike just lean enough for the scenario to be plausible. He probably weighed around two hundred and fifty pounds and the bike maybe three twenty-five or three fifty, so who knew?

"That's cool," I said, noncommittally.

"Yeah," he said, "I think so too." He picked up his helmet, one of those flared-rim iron Kaiser Wilhelm replicas, complete with top spike, and walked out. The bike looked flimsy underneath him as he kick-started it and rode off, like a circus gorilla on a tricycle.

"What an insane guy," I thought, and yet he's stayed in my mind all these years. When I started thinking about strength, he popped up right away as a perfect embodiment of raw physical power. I saw him clambering up the stairs of some East Village tenement with the motorcycle slung over his shoulder like a caveman and his girl. There was something absurd about it. Did he fuck the bike up the exhaust pipe? Or down the open air intake? Is that strength? I wondered.

I decided to ask my old high school Latin teacher, who'd long since retired and, after nursing his wife through a protracted and agonizing death, had become something of a neighborhood barfly. I found him on one of his usual stools, at a dive he frequented on Houston Street. He hadn't shaved in a few days and wore an old red flannel shirt. In front of him on the bar were a glass of whiskey, a short draft beer, and a pack of filterless Pall Mall cigarettes. He looked like the Platonic form of a wino.

"Hey! What are you doing here, kid?" he asked when I sat down. I told him what I wanted to ask him.

"Strength?" he asked. "What do I know about strength? Look at me. I'm plagued with hemorrhoids, my teeth are loose, and I can barely remember anything anymore. I'm afraid if I sneeze too hard, they'll find me wandering the streets in a toothless daze with blood and diarrhea dripping down my pants. Not exactly a role model, huh? I should be kicking the bucket any day now."

"Come on, Doc," I said, "quit being so dramatic. You're never going to die. Just gimme something to write for this article."

"I suppose from here on this stool, speaking as a stool specimen, as it were, I'd say that strength is youth. Not that youth is strength, but relatively speaking. Youth isn't necessarily young, you know? There's that beautiful expression in Tacitus's *Agricola* when he's describing the Scottish tribesmen who mustered to fight the Romans at Mons Graupius in 83 AD. Even the old men fought; or at least the ones who had what he calls a 'cruda et viridis senectus,' a 'raw and green old age.' I always loved that 'green old age,' viridis and virile. To be strong is to be green. The Romans didn't even have a word for middle age. There was youthful and then old, and it depended on that greenness, so a knotty, white-haired sixty-year-old ready for battle was younger than a fat thirty-year-old laid up with gout and venereal disease. Funny how that seems more real to me than the last fifteen years. Men who'd rather fight and die than submit to colonization and servility. Maybe that's what strength is. Holding out when you don't have a chance. Heedless of victory. Fuck it all."

He killed the whiskey in front of him and sighed.

"They lost, of course, but so what? They died free. Got a bit of the old Roman glory. In the end we all lose anyway: it all goes down the same damned hole. Carpe diem, kid. What are you having?"

XVIII

Another time we were in the studio, and I asked Dieter if he had any children. He didn't answer, and I thought maybe he hadn't heard me, but after a few minutes he said:

"No. No children."

A few more minutes passed, and he added

"Well, almost. But no. It was a nightmare."

He sank back into the picture, and I didn't say anything. I figured he'd tell me the story or not at some point or other, but then he went on.

"It's a long time ago, man. When I was about thirty, I fell in love really hard for a woman named Lina, from Argentina but German-Jewish family. She grew up speaking German. A killer, man, a poet. I used to think of her as a samurai. She was like one of those swords, and how she stood—she had some special power you could feel. She made people a little bit scared, you know, like she could see them. I don't know why she liked me. I wasn't such an exciting guy. It happened by accident, talking at a friend's house at a party after a funeral—some guy we both knew—with a lot of wine, and we left together and came back to the bar where I met you, stayed until the morning talking, and she came back to my place and that was it. We were together. A year and a half it was great, like a honeymoon. 'Moon honey' was a word she made up and said it was something we were drinking together. Like moonshine, but better. More sexual. Like we were drunk from sex all the time. And I painted her a lot. I liked so much just to sit together and talk and paint her, and maybe she was writing or reading or just looking out the window. When I saw her sleeping face, sometimes I thought I was going to go crazy, for no reason. Just because I couldn't believe she was there, and that she existed. But there was always something totally alone about her, like she was a survivor of something really bad, like a rape or a bad accident. I don't know, she would never say anything, but she had some big scars on her heart. Once I tried to ask her, and right away she almost bit me, said don't ask me that kind of thing, really angry, and I said fine, even though I wanted to know why. Maybe later she's gonna tell me, so ja, egal, whatever, man.

"OK, so we're together like that for a while, like a year and a half, really happy. Then she starts getting moody, little by little, more depressed. She wasn't writing anymore, and maybe that was making her a little crazy. Looking out the window like why bother. We're having fights about nothing. I kept asking her what's wrong, and she says nothing, but obviously she's lying. She doesn't want to talk, doesn't want to have sex anymore, doesn't even want to go out of the flat anymore. Just drifting away. So finally she tells me she wants to have a kid but she knows I don't want one, so that means she has to leave me or I'm gonna leave her. And it's driving her crazy, because she doesn't know why she wants to have a kid, but she feels it, like a thing, in her guts. And then other stuff, like where is the relationship going, I don't want to get married, I don't want to have children, what's the point, blah, blah, blah. I'm sure you heard this before. Universal female shit, man. Paradox. She loves me so much she's mad at me! Can you believe this? She loves me so much she wants to have a baby, and I don't want to, so she can't love me anymore. So that's gonna be it now: baby or get out. Man! All my life, I never wanted to have a kid. Not for any special reason, you know, I just didn't, didn't see the big deal, didn't want to change my life into this pattern, staying in the same place and taking care of a child. I'm a painter. That's what I'm doing. I don't have time for this kid stuff. Painter friends of mine who did it, they're not painters anymore. Then it becomes a hobby. Or they have to get a job. And when people are showing me the pictures of their kid, it's nice, but after five minutes, it's enough already. You go to their house, it's boring and noisy, toys and shit everywhere. So humanity can continue. Whatever, fine for them, I just didn't want it. It's egoistic, I know, but I liked my life. I didn't want to lose it. And I didn't want to lose her. It was fucked, man. Fucked if yes, fucked if no.

"So I tell her I need a little time to think about it, OK, baby?

And I do think about it. One day I'm out walking around on the Paul-Lincke-Ufer. I sit down and I'm watching some old guy feeding currywurst to the ducks down in the canal. He's breaking the little pieces of wurst in half and throwing them down into the water, and the ducks are swimming after them and shaking their heads back and forth when they get one and swallow it. Ducks eating meat, man! And this guy is watching them with this look on his face, like he's dreaming or maybe he's drunk. I wasn't sure, but his face was pink, and his nose, you know, it was a drunk-type nose, dark and purple with the veins. His clothes were old, but not like a homeless guy. Whatever. He seemed old and alone and lonely, left behind by life, just my feeling; maybe he had a wife and a house full of screaming children and came to the ducks for some quiet, but it looked like he was lonely and had nothing to do. At least, it fits my mood. And I'm thinking, am I gonna be this guy if I walk away from Lina now? Some dirty old guy with nobody, throwing cheap sausage at some ducks, like feeding the worms in your own grave before you die. I don't want to be sixty years old with a schnapps-burned nose and curry sauce on my fingers. And the ducks down there in that shitty water grabbing for the orange meat like it was something delicious—I don't know, my mind just switched and I said why not? I love her. I want her to be happy. I'm being selfish all my life. What's so great about how I'm living? All those people saying you don't understand anything until you have children. Maybe they're right. That kind of stuff. Something else inside me says, don't do it, man, don't do it for the wrong reason, but what's the wrong reason? The other voice says just say yes, all your life you thought too much about everything and then said no, so now why not just say yes once, stop thinking and say yes, make your old mamma a grandmother before she dies, have a life, be happy, blah, blah, blah. What do you call it, 'drinking the Kool-Aid'? I get a bottle of champagne and go home. I tell her, fuck it, I love her, let's have a baby. I'm happy. And she's happy too, not crazy, but she looks at me almost melancholic, with her big black eyes, and starts to cry and hugs me.

"OK. Fast-forward like you say. Some months of incredible fucking, like a new relationship, she gets pregnant. Life is good and now she's pregnant, so we're thinking about the future instead of the present. It's totally different—I don't know, when I was living in the present, even though I thought that was the best way to live, it was static, always the same, whether good or bad, like not moving, kind of numb, but only seemed to be moving, because even though nothing was happening, the years were going by. But now it's like looking ahead instead of staring at the ground by your feet: the future's coming and it's new life and you're part of it instead of watching it go by from the window while it's happening to other people. I didn't think of it before, but you get to a certain point and you feel like life has stopped happening to you, you know. You're stuck in the present, bored, getting older, and it's fucking dull. Soon you're gonna be just another bald guy with hemorrhoids. Maybe that's the trigger when it's time to have a kid. So now I felt like a tree, with new juices coming up in springtime. All simple stuff, all the clichés, you know, but when it's your cliché it's not a cliché anymore. I said to myself, you're gonna be one of those guys with a phone full of pictures of his most beautiful kid in the world, even if he looks like a fucking turtle. And Lina was so different too, so much more beautiful, like glowing, even so early. I don't know, man, it was like everything went from black and white to color. I know, another cliché.

"Then she lost it. In the bathroom one night, like eight, nine weeks. She felt sick, got up and went to the toilet, and that was it. She made this weird noise, not exactly a scream, but not good. I ran there, and she was sitting on the floor na-ked—she always slept naked—she's sitting there leaning on her side against the wall, not crying, quiet, with her eyes closed. Blood everywhere, on the toilet seat, the floor, all over her legs and hands. When she heard me, she opened her eyes and held out her hand to me. I thought she wanted me to hold it or help her, but no, like for me to take something, and then she drops this little wet thing in my hand. The fucking baby. A little thing; like a big red gummi bear on a string, translucent, but weird, weird proportions, big head, skinny little arms and legs, a fetus man. Even had tiny fingernails. Those fingernails killed me. I don't even know if it's true. I was staring at this thing in my hand, and I didn't know what to do. Paralyzed. Lina looked at me like a total stranger. Then it was like some shadow passed over her face, this blink in her eyes, and she gets up, walked to the bedroom, got dressed, and walked out of the flat. She didn't even wipe the blood off herself. Pulled her blue jeans on right over it, then her boots, and out the door. And I was standing there with the dead baby in my hand. What the fuck am I supposed to do? Flush it down the toilet and run after her? Leave it there? I had the sudden idea of a rat eating it, biting his head and sucking the brain like a candy, even though we didn't have any rats in the flat. Put it in the refrigerator? It's so strange what your mind can think of in a situation like this. I knew I should go for her, but for some reason I couldn't. Like I said, I was paralyzed. Where the fuck did she go? I sat on the bloody toilet and cried like a baby. First time I'm crying since I was a kid.

"She came back in the morning. Never told me where she went. But she was different, back to the depression, but a million times worse. No talking, no touching, nothing. I put my hand on her shoulder, she drops it and moves away like a snake. In bed, forget it. I reach over to hold her, and again she moves away. Just keeps moving away. Sometimes she even says please not to touch her. I'm like, Lina, it's me, baby. I'm not your enemy, it's gonna be better, we can do it again, I'm here, we'll have a baby, please, just talk to me, and then she says no, it's not gonna be better, that this is the third time, it's a curse, she's useless, her pussy is a black hole. She said this, my pussy is a black hole. I'm shit. Pretty bad, man, but I'm thinking time fixes everything, right? I hope. She'll get over it. I told her I'm not going anywhere, you hear me, I love you, and I'm staying right here. You're never getting rid of me. So it's like two, three months, no change, I start to think maybe she needs to talk to somebody, like a professional, but forget it she says, it's fucking bullshit, some asshole Freud gonna talk her cunt back to life? Fuck off! She just stays at home, sleeping most of the time, or lying in bed watching movies. It was horrible, just coming apart. Sometimes she would stare at herself in the mirror like she couldn't remember who she was. Her face got skinny and pale. She's smoking all the time. Taking sleeping pills. I don't even know where she was getting them. Drinking too. A couple of pills and a wineglass of vodka and then staying in bed for another fucking fourteen hours.

"So then one time I have to go away to Hamburg for the weekend, for a show in a gallery there where I'm gonna have two paintings. Of course she won't come. But she wants me to go, get out of Berlin for a couple of days. It's good for me. She wants to be alone for a little. OK. Maybe I just stay one night, come back the next day after the opening. I was a little nervous to go, but I went. I call her that night, no answer. I called her a few times, same thing. I'm like, shit, baby, come on, answer the phone. I think, those fucking sleeping pills. I'm getting sick of it, man. The opening's cool. I sold one painting right away, a nice girl coming at me, young Blondine, red lips, nice tits, nipple rings I can see through a ripped Pauli T-shirt. I like her, you know, I'm thinking Lina doesn't give a fuck about sex anymore, I'm gonna have a little fun with this one. Fuck, it's nice to feel something, you know? I wanna get laid. So I do, with the Blondine. She comes to my hotel, we play around a little while. It's fun, but I'm a little bored and miss Lina. I felt worried, wondering what the fuck she's doing. I decide I'm gonna go back on the first train in the morning. Blondine leaves.

"In the morning I call Lina to tell her I'm coming back. I wanna take her for a nice dinner, I miss her, I love her. I want to tell her all this stuff, but again she doesn't answer the phone.

OK. Train ride back, some more calls, still nothing. Maybe she's mad I left, but now I'm getting a little mad too. How long am I supposed to take this shit? Maybe if I leave, she will get some help finally. So I get home, depressed as fuck, thinking maybe I even need to get out of Europe for a while, whatever. I open the door, and it's very quiet. I call her, 'Lina, it's me, Lina, you here?' No answer."

He stopped talking for a moment, took a deep drag on the cigarette, and stared at the painting. Then he sighed slowly and exhaled a long cloud of smoke.

"Yeah, man. She killed herself while I was gone. And she did it like a samurai—no chance for me to find her still alive. I found her in the bathtub in a pool of cold bloody water with her eyes closed, like a horrible frozen princess. She cut her wrists, plus a bottle of pills. It was the pills that really killed her. I think the blood was just for the picture. The water in the tub was so disgusting. Thick and disgusting. With scum on the surface. A note on the table said I'm sorry for everything. I love you. Please forgive your useless black hole.

"After that I was pretty fucked up for a while. A lot of drinking, cocaine. Just vodka, cocaine, and painting. I wanted to die by a heart attack with a paintbrush in my hand, painting a picture of Lina. A bit melodramatisch, I know.

"But then a funny thing. I had a great nose for cocaine. I could tell how pure it was, what it was cut with, like I had a fucking electric meter in my head. My dealer was amazed. He started to test me for fun, and I was always getting the right answer. Which is better, more expensive. So one day he says to me, hey man, I want you to work with me as a taster. You

come with me when I'm buying and check how good the mer-
chandise is, like my advisor, or what's the word, 'consultant.'
Ja, so now I'm a 'cocaine consultant'—going to coke deals in
the most expensive hotels in Berlin with these Turkish gangster
guys. Ridiculous man, totally absurd, the whole thing, black
suits, sunglasses, arrive in the black Mercedes, briefcases full
of cash and drugs, guns on the table. It's like they're copying
the movies. I'm thinking, which one is real? Or am I in the
movies now? I sniff lines of everything they got, like six, seven
lines in four, five minutes, super pure shit, some not. I'm out
of my mind, my head's like a beehive, but I can still stay cool,
just stay behind the sunglasses, lean over and mumble in my
dealer's ear. No problem. I get some money and all the coke
I need. My commission, you call it, yeah? Then I'm back in
my studio painting. It was strange. I was getting fucked up
to forget, but painting these pictures to remember. I had this
same picture in my mind all the time, Lina in the bath with
her eyes open and her tits floating in a puddle of thick, black
blood, like a swamp. Frogs and snails and huge flies sitting on
the edge of the bathtub, licking and sucking the blood loud
enough to hear it. The flies slurping the blood. A big, slimy eel
rolled up in her mushy, sticking his head out. I was going crazy,
man. The coke was making me crazy. I didn't sleep for days at a
time. Just painting the same picture all the time, over and over,
like printing from the negative in my mind. In three months,
I made like twenty-five of them, black hole number one, black
hole number two, etc. Blah blah blah. In the mirror, I look like
Nosferatu, with two red holes in his face and another hole full
of yellow teeth. My skin was gray and wrinkled, like newspa-

per. I wasn't doing good, man. I ate almost nothing, a coffee in the morning. I didn't really even shit anymore, maybe once or twice a week, some green liquid, like some weird kind of bird shit, squirt it out, fah! like a chicken. Like my ass was spitting. Then one day I missed the appointment for the coke deal. I just forgot. At this time, I didn't know anymore which day of the week it was, so I missed it, and this is the day they got busted, man. Can you believe it? Busted. Prison for everybody. Pure luck I didn't go there. And thank God they knew who the rat was, some guy on the other side, or it wouldn't look good for me.

"But that's what woke me up. Just that piece of luck. I was like, I gotta stop this shit right now. I'm almost dead. I destroyed all the paintings. I smashed them and burned them in a trash can and left that apartment. Got this place. I still think about Lina all the time, but just sad now, not crazy, and the picture is not in my mind anymore. The fucked-up thing is now I almost can't remember what she looked like. I have to look at a photo sometimes to remind me. My mind is like an empty room with a fuzzy picture of her on the wall."

XIX

My thirty-first birthday was approaching, and I was living in Venezuela, so we planned a little party Venezuelan-style, or rather El Salado, Margarita Island-style: kill a goat, make a stew, play cards, and drink whiskey, eat the stew, play more cards, and drink more whiskey. A "sancocho party": *sancocho* means stew. Usually, it would be a chicken or two or some fish, but this was a special occasion—the gringo's birthday, so a goat.

The goat belonged to Gustavo's cousin Elys Carmen and was living in her backyard, but she didn't like him and was happy to get rid of him in exchange for a sheep, a placid, fatter animal she preferred to have around. Plus, she'd like the wool, she said, so we got her a sheep. The day before we were going to eat the goat, I went over there to see him and have a little chat. I don't know why, really, but it seemed like a good idea. I guess I felt a little guilty and wanted to ease my conscience by acknowledging him. He was a pure black billy, with curving horns and a scraggly beard, standing behind a wire fence and chewing on a mouthful of scrub. I walked up to him, right into his smell.

There's nothing quite like the smell of goat musk. It's a rank haze that tickles your nose with its texture, vibrating somewhere between a sour smell and a buzzing sound—hard to describe, but if you've smelled it, you know what I mean. He stood there chewing, dipping his head down every now and again to pull up another bite. The weeds went slowly into his mouth, sucked in by the action of his relentless nibbling. Sorry, man, I thought. Tomorrow we're going to kill you. I'm not a vegetarian. I like goat meat. That's just the way it goes. Maybe it'll be different in the next life, if there is one. I know—that's easy for me to say. It was very hot, over 100 degrees, and after a few minutes he stopped eating and pointed his face downward into his crotch. His penis emerged, a long, pink stalk with a small, flat cap flaring at the end of it, like some strange giraffe mushroom. He put his face up in front of it and started to piss on himself, lapping up and drinking the piss as it spritzed him. I guess his mouth was dry from all the heat and weeds. The musk smell intensified.

"All right," I said to him, trying but unable to find an allegory in this, "I'll call you scape. Tomorrow we're gonna cut your throat and eat you. Enjoy your last day."

I left him there, basking in his acrid cloud.

Later that day we booked the services of Juan Chiria, who was famous around there for the deliciousness of his stews, running marathons barefoot, and his immoderate love of iguana meat. There was even a little song about that:

Juan Chiria buscaba iguana
alla por el Fallardón
si no me como iguana
me como camaleón!

Juan Chiria was hunting iguana
down there by el Fallardón
if I don't eat me an iguana
I'll eat me some chameleón!

We drove up into the hills behind the town, found his hovel, and banged on the chipped, turquoise-blue door. A dark-haired girl of about fifteen with a baby propped on her hip opened the door. She looked at us with large black eyes and sullen curiosity. More children scampered around behind her in the shadow of the room. We said we were looking for Juan, who it turned out was both her father, we heard later, and the father by her of the baby she held in her arms. All told, said a friend, he had fourteen children, most of them grown, and had fathered three of his own grandchildren. Juan came to the door, a spry, leathery man of about sixty-five in a sleeveless undershirt and dirty brown slacks, his face missing a front tooth and speckled with gray stubble. His eyes were glazed and bloodshot. He was holding a brown bottle of beer beaded with condensation. When we told him we wanted him to cook a stew the following day, he was delighted. His face lit up.

"Fantastico!" he cried with a sudden squawk, like an alarmed chicken. "But you gotta get me some things." And he listed the ingredients: Worcestershire sauce, ketchup, onions, garlic, sugar, rum, three cases of beer …

The next day we went up to Bocho's house in the mountains. It was more of a high-end shack, really, on a flat slab of tiled concrete in an undeveloped stretch of rocky orange dirt and parched vegetation. He called it Las Delicias, an old Spanish expression meaning "my delight" and always in the plural. He had a small tiled pool, just big enough for four or five people to sit in, and water ran into it from a fountain spout in the shape of a satyr's mask. It made a soothing, cooling sound.

Juan Chiria was already waiting there with an assistant named Miguelito. They'd set up his cooking area next to large brick barbecue and watched us without moving as we arrived. We had the ingredients, the beer, some whiskey. The goat tied up in the trunk of the car. Miguelito unloaded it all, laying the goat on his side a few yards from the grill. The goat lifted his head, bleating with indignation at his bound ankles, rocking back and forth as he tried to get up and failed. We drank a couple of beers while they arranged the ingredients. Then Miguelito picked up a knife, bent over the goat, pulled his scrotum out through his bound hind legs, and sliced it off. The goat gave one sharp cry as his flesh was cut, then went strangely silent, as if he knew it was over already, lying sideways and bleeding out a puddle of bright, cherry-colored blood. The blood expanded slowly over the tile.

"Pobrecito," said Juan Chiria, abstractedly, sipping a beer. Miguelito tossed the scrotum into the dirt, flinging it away with a flick of his wrist. A few drops of blood flew off. I remember thinking it reminded me of an ear, a severed human ear.

"How long you going to let him bleed like that?" I asked, after about ten minutes went by. "Aren't you gonna kill him?"

Juan Chiria seemed amused by my squeamishness.

"Half an hour," he said, "while I make everything. Don't worry about that, chico. It doesn't hurt him so much. That's how it's done. Because his smell is in the belly, all around the balls. If you don't bleed it out, the meat tastes like piss. Then it's a waste. Remember that for next time."

Juan Chiria had the beginnings of his sauce going in a large stew pot which he was stirring with an old barkless stick. He called me over and held it up, showing me where he'd honed it flat at the bottom "so it stirs better. La paleta magica!" He grinned: the magic spoon. "That's what gives my stew its incredible flavor!" Su sabor increíble. "You'll see, chico, you'll see!" He cackled like some strange South American leprechaun; then his smile faded, and he returned to stirring his stew.

And it all went according to Juan Chiria's plan. Half an hour later, he grabbed the goat by the horns and bent his head forward, and Miguelito smacked him behind the ears with a section of rebar, smashing his skull and killing him instantly. They skinned him and butchered him into pieces, braised and stewed and stirred them with the magic spoon to a sweet brown viscosity, and that night we feasted on him, with laughter and whiskey and cards under an open, star-splattered sky. Tree frogs and crickets peeping and seething. An ancient sacrifice for my pagan birthday.

XX

It's strange to be American and Jewish in Germany. Like everywhere, it's two things, not one, and if Germans think you might be Jewish, at some point they'll ask you. If you are, that new knowledge will affect your relationship, make it a bit more delicate. The past is still there, and though almost everyone directly involved is dead by now, no one knows how to deal with it. What are you supposed to do? Should I go around thinking maybe that guy's great-grandfather killed my grandmother's cousin in Poland somewhere? Should Germans still feel guilty and Jews hate or fear them? Must we all carry these ancestral national emotions? It doesn't make sense, and it does, like a lot of superstitious thinking, but that's what *superstitious* means, something from the past that's left over, still standing.

Seventy-five years ago, I'd have been running for my life from the Nazis. A partisan or packed on a livestock train toward slavery and extermination. Jews were the enemy of the Race State, immoral, rootless cosmopolitans. We were friends, neighbors, lovers one day, the next day parasitical vermin. Untermenschen. Interracial sex between Germans and Jews was a crime, polluting the Aryan, Übermenschen gene pool, the blue-eyed blond mirage. Now I'm a mildly exotic foreigner, gilded with the guilt of the past.

You almost have to admire those terms: *Übermenschen* and *Untermenschen*—overman and underman. Why beat around the bush, right? The famed German efficiency—even in language, compressing the racism and contempt into prefixes, as if it were merely structural, and maybe it actually is: A over B, the syntax of fratricide. But in this case, it's also a parody of a sexual pair, top and bottom, and sometimes I think it's true that Germans and Jews derive a sick, pseudo-sexual historical glamor from one another: the Germans as the ultimate sadists, evil, methodical killers, perpetrators of the "greatest atrocity in history," and the Jews as the ultimate victims, masochistic lambs, the "chosen people" singled out for destruction. Leatherboy SS über with bullwhip and chaps, emaciated unter submissive in striped pajamas and clogs. Anyway, it's a lot more interesting than being French or Italian. And for the most part now the Jews are white people. We got promoted, got a country; we even have our own Untermenschen to dispossess and revile. I guess times have changed. But it hasn't been that long, and who knows how long it will last?

I was in this jazz bar in Neu Köln one night, a kind of run-down, kitschy, neo-goth Americana East Village living-room joint, with velvet-relief wallpaper and candelabra-style light fixtures mounted on the walls. The bartender was a guy about sixty, named Mark who looked like a gray-haired Nick Cave impersonator with long sideburns and a prominent upturned nose that allowed you to see into his nostrils. I was sitting with a few musicians at the bar. It was late. We were drinking a lot of cheap red wine and chain-smoking cigarettes, everyone rolling them by hand and talking, hash going around as well, and one thing led to another, the free jazz scene in Berlin, some musician gossip, the election of Donald Trump, and, of course, Hitler. Genocide. Some half-assed intimations that perhaps America was sliding toward fascism. The Standing Rock protest was happening just then in North Dakota, November, 2016. They wanted to know what I thought, since I was the only American there. I tell them, that shit's why I'd rather be here. I just don't want to deal with it, you know what I mean? Well, obviously you think about it or you wouldn't be upset, they said, so why don't you just say what's on your mind? We're curious. Alright, I said, feeling the booze begin to unfurl my tongue, it does make me upset. It's embarrassing. The Standing Rock thing? It's like the 19th century, when the railroads were being built through whatever was left of native territory, the same shit all over again, just with pipelines instead of rails, corporate imperial greed plowing through indigenous subhumanity. And they're subhuman because they're there, colored, in the way. Underfoot. Untermenschen. Manifest Destiny. Did they know this term? Not really. So I continued pontificating. Manifest Destiny was the divinely ordained right of the white Christian American Übermensch to take possession of everything until California. It was kind of like Lebensraum. Deschwartzifikation. Exterminate and annex. Hitler knew his American history. He even said he admired the way the Americans gunned millions of redskins down to a few hundred thousand kept in cages. Hans Frank called the Ukrainian Jews Indians.

There was some indignant grumbling among them at that line, but Hitler's always a touchy subject in Germany. Especially when foreigners swing him around. Hey, I said, you guys brought it up. We were way ahead of you in eugenics and race law until the mid-thirties, when you finally got going. But think about it from Hitler's point of view. He saw that America got away with it, expanded all the way west, wiped out the natives and enjoyed African slavery for centuries. Why couldn't he do it with continental Europe and Russia? Wipe out the Jews, assimilate the Aryan Nordics, and enslave the Slavs? The word *slave* even comes from Slav—like it was their etymological destiny. (Eyebrows raised in skeptical admiration at this point. Really? Wirklich?)

What distinguished the Germans in genocide is what distinguishes you in everything, I went on. Rationality, precision, efficiency. If you're gonna do something, do it right. You weren't hypocrites about it. We said all men are created equal and had slavery. You guys said, no, we are the superior master race and will kill or enslave the inferior. No more compunction than one swarm of insects wiping out another. That's what's amazing. You calculated everything, the railway links right into the camps, the ventilation and convection requirements of the gas chambers and ovens, even stripping people's hair to make felt and melting gold teeth back to ingots. House shoes made from Jewish women's hair. Auschwitz could gas and burn nine thousand people a day. Compared to that, Gatling guns and infected blankets look like stone-age, amateur bullshit.

You think about it, I said, a concentration camp is just the logical endpoint of capitalism. Slave labor, worked to death, no wages, no benefits, no freedom, the absolute minimum to survive, and when they can't work anymore, you kill them. It's a perfect corporate model. Ultimate deregulation. The Volkswagen plant used to be a concentration camp, for fuck's sake. They had twelve different slave camps. Strength through Joy City. Worktown. They even recruited workers from Auschwitz, the ones too valuable to waste too soon over there. Don't you think modern corporations would do that if they could get away with it? They even had slogans like Arbeit macht frei, or jedem das Seine—to each his own. Or the name *Vernichtungslager*-annihilation camp—it's the perfect name for a beer. "Vernichtunglager, when Arbeit makes you fry." Imagine if you'd won! But you blew it, and now you've had to eat shit for decades. You were the worst people in history, and so on. What's weird is now you guys are becoming the good guys, and the Americans are starting to look like the insane, racist assholes of history.

Things were getting a little out of hand, and people seemed uncomfortable, watching me wide-eyed in silence as I raved.

You're not supposed to talk like that in Germany. Only when there's a lot of alcohol, and afterward everyone can forget or pretend to forget what was said. Finally Mark hit the gavel. "Man, I think it might be time to close up now. It's five o'clock in the morning, okay? Let's just get out of here and go home." So we did, into the last of the night, sidewalks splattered with broken glass and dogshit. The birds were already twittering somewhere up in the blackness.

XXI

On the morning of 9-11 I was still in bed when my mother called me and said turn on your TV, in a dull voice which struck me. She didn't say my name or hello, or anything, and normally she's so talkative, she launches into a torrent of babbling as soon as I say hello. So I turned it on and saw the image of the punctured towers, huge plume of smoke snaking out horizontally like a dragon over lower Manhattan. I could have seen it from my window because I lived in Williamsburg at the time, with a view of the skyline from the kitchen, but like most people, even New Yorkers, I still saw it first on TV. I grabbed a pair of binoculars and ran up one flight to the roof of my building, and there it was, right across the river. I could see through the binoculars an airplane tail hanging out of the south tower and flame cascading through the gash, tumbling down like a waterfall. I couldn't believe it. I just sat there transfixed, watching the smoke and flame through the binoculars, I don't know, maybe twenty minutes, until the tower seemed to start wobbling and then the corner tipped forward a little and the whole thing collapsed into itself in an avalanche of billowing ash and smoke. The building disappeared into the cloud. I didn't know what was going on at the scene, but I thought at least fifty thousand people must have died in that instant. It was 10 a.m.

You never know how you're going to react to a thing like that. I went back downstairs into my apartment and started trashing it, throwing things around, books mostly, hurling them into walls, smashed a few baubles, a vase, a photo frame, which seems like a pretty stupid thing to do. I guess I panicked. I didn't know what else to do, but it was stupid and pointless. While I was there doing that, the second tower collapsed, which again I saw on TV, in instant replay, over and over, a plummeting fountain of ashes. I ran back up onto the roof, and the entire bottom of Manhattan was lost in a cloud of white and gray and black smoke expanding and drifting slowly southeastward on the wind. Some other people were there on the roof as well, but nobody said anything. We stood there leaning on the wall and watching the smoke in a blank reverie, like we'd seen a volcano erupting, a vast, stupefying disaster.

It seems like so long ago, but it's only so many years.

XXII

Back then, I was a street photographer and used to work around the Port Authority Bus Terminal in Manhattan. Mostly, I walked up and down Eighth and Ninth Avenues between about 36th and 48th Streets, which in those days was full of people scraping their living off the streets, a lot of panhandling, hooking, drug dealing. There were even three-card monte and bottlecap shell games being played on stacks of cardboard boxes. Times Square and 42nd Street were still the porno district, and the bus station was a magnet for drifters with nowhere else to go: drunks, addicts, runaways and strays, people waiting around for something to happen as an endless tide of commuters washed in and around the building. There was a wild-eyed preacher from Oklahoma I remember who told me God had come to him and ordered him to leave the prairie and go to Times Square to preach His word for the conversion and salvation of souls. That was how he said it, "for the conversion and salvation of souls." I'd guess he was around seventy, gaunt, with shoulder-length, thin gray hair receding from a high forehead. He always wore a clean white shirt, white cowboy boots with pale blue jeans tucked in, and a leather string tie with a quarter-sized turquoise medallion framed in silver. When the Spirit moved him, he stood on the southeast corner of 42nd Street and Eighth Avenue looking up at the sky and shouting about the revelation. When the Spirit didn't move him, and he had his pension money, he'd pick up one of the young male prostitutes who worked the southwest corner across the street outside the station. That old man likes to suck dick, one of them told me. I still have his picture somewhere, mid-harangue, with mouth wide open, head tilted back, and glossy black eyes that were somehow both dead and ablaze, like a furious old shark sinking his teeth into Satan's vicious thigh.

One person I photographed often was a transvestite prostitute, a petite Filipino in her mid-twenties who called herself Coco.

At first she thought I was a john. I was walking around looking for pictures with a similarly hungry eye when she came up to me, put her arm into mine without breaking my stride, and walked along, leaning into me like a girlfriend. "Come with me, honey," she said, "I'll blow you out of this world!" She winked and licked her lips.

"No thanks," I said, "not my thing. But I'd love to take your picture. Would you mind?"

The idea seemed to amuse her. She paused and looked me up and down, lingering a moment on my boots.

"Normally I'd say no," she said, "but you're cute. Why not?"

She propped herself against the brick wall of a building we were passing and began to pose, pouting her lips, tilting and tossing her head and running her fingers through her hair like a seasoned model. She took a pair of pink lace panties out of her jacket and began pulling them around, stretching the leg holes in front of her face and looking through the opening, bending her knees and stooping forward with a variety of co-quettish smiles and suggestive expressions. It was an amazing display, and she kept it up for about fifteen minutes. I shot three rolls of film, black-and-white Kodak Tri-XPan, thirty-six frames per roll.

"Thanks," I said.

"Well, now you owe me a coffee at least," she said and winked.

"Anywhere you like," I said, and that's how it began.

Sometimes she liked to walk up and down Ninth Avenue with me, arm in arm, leaning her head on my shoulder and babbling stories about her life on the streets. Often, they were horrible, but she always told them in a light–hearted, chat-tering way, like a little girl recounting things that happened to her at school with the other children. The beat cops didn't like seeing us like that, as if it offended their sense of propriety somehow, and they always made a point of telling me Coco was a man, as if they wanted to scare me off and leave her emp-ty-handed. Mostly white and young, looking like rookies pink scrubbed and fresh from the academy. Sometimes they would even interrupt me when I photographed her, saying things like, "You know that's a dude, right?" But after a while, they got used to me and gave up trying. They never let me photograph them though.

One day I ran into her outside the hotel she lived in, a nasty shambles of a place on the corner of 47th and Eighth. I think it was called the Sherman Hotel. Coco's eye was full of blood, the surrounding cheek and socket caked with makeup badly masking a bruise.

"What happened?" I asked.

"This asshole," she said. "He came by my room looking for a blowjob, and while I was doing him, he reached down to grab my crotch. When he felt my dick there, he flipped out, started screaming fucking faggot this, fucking queer that, Jesus Christ. Slapped me a few times. Took one really good swing and got me. It's OK. I know how to find him. I'll cut that motherfucker's dick off. But I'll plan my revenge. He doesn't know who he messed with."

She invited me up to her room, which was a bare cubicle with a bed in the middle that took up most of the room. There was nowhere else to sit but on the bed. We sat down. I snapped a few funny close-ups and some of her lounging on her belly, chin propped in her hand and one leg jauntily up in the air. Reflections of her and the flaking paint walls in a cracked triangular fragment of mirror. She reached into her bag and pulled out a glass pipe and a plastic crack vial, a clear little hexagonal tube with a bright red stopper, fixed it, and lit up. She offered me some, but I said no. I didn't know until that moment that she smoked it, because she showed none of the obvious signs. I was surprised.

It hit her and she transformed, starting into a megalomaniac rant. She was a goddess, she was the sun, no one knew who she was, but they'd find out soon. I kept shooting her. Her eyes were lit with a sickly glow. She blinked furiously, and a muscle in her cheek twitched in spasms. She was a poet, she went on, an angel being punished for disobedience. Her wings were clipped, but just for now. She would be reborn from the ashes of alpha and omega, with golden skin and champagne flowing through her veins. Did I know what a phoenix was? Tatonzhay, baby! Of course I did. I was the only one who could see it. This was why she'd chosen me to photograph her. She'd chosen me and would make me famous. We were a divine pair, had known each other before, angel lovers from another universe and time.

She was sitting on her knees and bouncing up and down on the mattress as she said all this. Then she took another hit, grabbed my head and pulled it to her, kissed me on the lips and blew the smoke into my lungs. I inhaled it out of curiosity, but it was second hand and just made me a little jittery.

"Now you must fuck me!" she said and pulled off her shirt. Her pectorals were like small female breasts, with fleshy brown nipples.

"No, Coco," I said. "I'm not gonna do that. Come on."

Her face turned into an angry scowl.

"What?" she shouted. "You dare to refuse me? I'm talking

for free! You refuse me? You know what people pay for this out there, you stupid piece of shit? Get out of here! Get the fuck out of here now!"

She was screaming. She picked up her shoe and held it with the tip of the heel pointed at me as if she wanted to drive it into my skull.

"All right," I said. "I'm out of here."

I left and went back out to the street.

After that, I didn't see her for a while. Maybe she was avoiding me. Maybe not. Whenever we'd met, it was always by chance anyway. In those days no one had cell phones. Now it seems like antiquity.

Winter was coming on and it got cold. There were fewer people on the streets, and they were turned inward more, huddling into collars and doorways. The streets were windy and bleak, the sunlight harsh and white. I'd got a teaching job upstate that would start in January and only had a few more weeks before leaving. Finally, I ran into Coco one morning looking haggard and drawn, downcast. None of her usual magnetic, flirtatious energy. She asked me to have a coffee with her, but she wanted to sit outside on a brownstone stairway. I bought two coffees, and we went and sat down.

"Where you been, baby? I haven't seen you around."

"I've been around," I said. "I haven't seen you either. I thought you might have been avoiding me."

"Me?" she asked, putting her hand on her sternum, "How could I avoid you, baby? You know I adore you."

"I don't know. That last time in your room it got a little weird. You seemed pretty angry."

"Oh. That was nothing. Sometimes I just go a little cuckoo on the c, that's all. Forget about that, please."

"I'm leaving soon, Coco. I got a job upstate, teaching."

"Teaching what? Where?"

"Upstate New York. At a college out in dairy country. I won't be around for a while."

"I thought you were a photographer. What about the pictures? They're so beautiful."

"Thanks. I'm glad you like them, but they're not paying any bills. I need the job. Anyway, it's just temporary. I'll be back in a few months, in May or June. Will you still be here?"

When I saw the look on her face, I realized what a stupid question that was, the infinite gap that yawned between us. As if she had a choice.

"I don't know," she said. "You never know out here. Maybe my ship will come in, or maybe some fucking demon will kill me. Or maybe I'll still be right here, walking the streets. One day at a time."

She laughed, then looking at me very seriously, in a quiet voice, said, "Take me with you. I'll be anything you like. Your lover, your houseboy, your slave. I'll cook for you and clean for you. I mean it. Just take me away from here. Get me out of this shit for a while."

"Where are you from, Coco? You have anywhere to go back to? Maybe I could help you, get you a ticket …"

"I'm from the Philippines but grew up in Thailand. I'll never go back there. When I was six, my father started selling me to Germans. Rich pederasts on holiday, three weeks or a month at a time. It was disgusting. They kept me in their bungalows and raped me, like fat pigs. Then sat me on their laps and fed me by hand like a pet. But that's how my family ate. When I was ten, I ran away to Bangkok and worked as a whore till I was sixteen, seventeen. I don't even know when my birthday is. So I chose today, January tenth, the day Coco Chanel died. Happy birthday, huh?

"A guy fell in love with me, a queer American lawyer on holiday, lots of money. He was totally crazy about me, wanted to bring me here, put me in an apartment. I said of course, baby, New York? Everybody's dream. So I came. I had a little place over by the tunnel on Eleventh, shitty but mine. First time in my life I could lock the door and no one could bother me. I had a bathtub! And an allowance. He bought me nice things. I was a kept little boy. I had everything I needed. When he wanted me, we went to hotels, fancy ones, drank champagne, bubble baths. The rest of my time was my own. He was nice, actually. I guess I even loved him a little. He took care of me. But totally in the closet. Married, kids, the whole deal. Then the wife found out, and it was over. Just like that. I was nothing. Out in the cold again.

My real name is Raymond Castro. You believe that? A Spanish colonial name for this little brown piece of trash. I'm twenty-four. I never had anything to sell but my ass. I've been used my whole life, and there's nowhere to go from here but down. I'm not gonna be this beautiful forever, baby."

She smiled coquettishly, back in character for a second, then back out.

"I'm serious. I'll do anything for you, everything. Just take me with you. Have you ever had a better offer in your life?"

I didn't take her with me. I went upstate and taught at a college in dairy country, Virgil and Sophocles in a place that felt like a golf club for adolescents. It didn't seem to make much sense. I thought about the kids I taught. I thought about myself, and Coco. What was I doing there?

It was cold, with a lot of snow, and I spent the days when I wasn't teaching driving around in the desolate white hills photographing dilapidated barns and trailers. A classic image began to emerge, like a coin or a stamp, definitely an emblem: trailer set back parallel to the road, on one side a satellite dish pointed up to the sky, on the other a pick-up parked at an oblique angle, maybe a defined driveway, paved or dirt, maybe not. Sometimes a house-like doublewide with a mud room add-on or a flagpole in a ring of white stones, others slouching and decayed, with burnt-out cars and appliances littering the property. Fading red and yellow plastic toys. Endlessly bleak snow-covered hills rolling in every direction for miles and miles.

After three months the snow thawed and spring began to appear in patches of mud and dead yellow grass. Another month later it was full-blown spring and I was gone, back down to New York City. I took my camera and went back to the Port Authority, walked around looking for Coco, the Preacher, or anyone else I knew from before, but I didn't find a single one. Everyone was gone.

XXIII

I met this girl named Julie at an art opening. She was a French photographer with a fetish for big beards, or so her friend, another photographer I'd just met that day, informed me as soon as she'd left us to go get a glass of wine. I had a big beard, and he told me she would be all over me if I let her. I was exactly her type: tall, wiry, a bit grizzled, a bit on the ugly side, if you asked him, but in a rugged sort of way. That was her thing, man. Sure enough, a few days later she sent me an email. She was working on a project about beards and their owners and would like to photograph me. Would I mind? Of course not, I replied. What would it involve? A few days later, I went over to her studio, and she shot me for a couple of hours. There was something open and beautiful about her, her large, deep blue eyes and smile, and we were very at ease with each other. It was a hot summer day, and we were in the studio for part of the time and part of the time up on her rooftop with a view over the low-slung stretches of Bushwick and Bed-Stuy. Afterward, she took me for drinks to some rock and roll hipster bar on Broadway called Lone Wolf, and we got drunk and ended up back in bed at her place, laughing and screwing for a couple of hours and falling asleep. In the morning, we exchanged numbers, thanks, it was lovely, hope the pictures are good, maybe see you again some time, yes, okay, and I left.

A couple of weeks later, she called. I want you to fuck me on your kitchen table, she says. Just like that. Strip me, lift me up and put me down on my back, then get up on the table and fuck me. Is this an obscene phone call? I teased her. Yes, she said, I want you to rub your beard on my breasts and fuck me like a whore on your table. Ok, I said. Jump in a cab and come over. I gave her my address, which was just a few minutes away.

The kitchen table was a little high and on wheels, more of an antique cart than a table, actually—a little impractical for what she wanted—so I fucked her against the counter, from behind, with her head in the sink, then on the floor, on a small dirty rug, in a sparse rubble of food bits and cat litter, all the while hoping my housemate/landlord would not come home and walk in on this picture-perfect, caught-with-your-pants-down humping going on in front of the dishwasher. That would have been awkward, but luckily not. Julie seemed satisfied. As she was leaving, she asked to read my book *Exit Bag*, which I'd mentioned when she was photographing me. She said she was traveling the next day and wanted something to read on the plane, so I gave it to her, an email, since it hadn't been published. It's a little crude, I told her. Been rejected many times. But you can read it if you want to. That's what I tell anyone nice enough to be curious.

A week later she calls from Colorado to tell me the book made her cry. She wanted to scream. She wants me to love her the way the narrator loved Maite, the main female character in the book, even though I wrote about that as if it were a form of insanity. Something destructive and undesirable, better to be free of. It's a novel, I tell her. It's inherently unreal. Exaggerated for artistic purposes. It's not even published. Bullshit, she says, I know that was real, and hangs up.

She came back, and over the next couple of months we slept together a few times, casually. A once-in-a-while, mutually agreed upon booty-call type thing. Then one day she attacked. We were sitting outside having a beer when she turned to me and snapped:

"You know what? You're an asshole."

"What?" I said.

Then a stream of complaints. I don't love her. I just want to fuck her, use her, I've never cared about her, just want her body. I never suggest we do anything fun like go to a museum together or the movies, or even take a walk. Do I realize we've never even gone out for a nice dinner? No. Of course I don't. Just fuck. An asshole. A fucking asshole, literally. Who do I think I am anyway? She doesn't want to see me anymore. Ever. I can just forget it, and so on. All of a sudden, in her mind I've hurt her, even though she took the initiative at every step. Why? I wanted to say. Why do you have to pull this shit and ruin everything? Something fun, free, and beautiful, like a couple of dolphins playing in the sea. What happened to the fuck-me-on-the-kitchen-table stuff? Were the blowjobs just a ploy to enslave me? Why do you have to domesticate me into a boyfriend? And why do you have to make me into the bad guy? Just because I like sex without attachment? Does that mean I should go to prostitutes? Or masturbate in public like Diogenes? I thought we had an understanding ...

There was more I wanted to say, but I didn't say any of it. What good would it do? It seems to be an eternal conflict. One wants more than the other, regardless of male or female.

"I'm sorry you feel that way," I said, and I was. "But I don't want to be in a contest of wills. I didn't think that that's what this was about."

"Then fuck you," she said. And that was the end of it.

XXIV

I saw this video of an old Italian man lying on his back in the sun in a small wooden rowboat. He was shirtless, dangling his legs over the side and smoking a cigarette as the boat rocked gently back and forth. His white hair and tan skin, the crystal-clear, turquoise blue of the water, almost as if it weren't even there, as if the boat were floating in an insubstantial azure. I think it was somewhere in Sardegna. If ever there were an image of carpe diem, it was there. How different from all our frenzied talk of improvement and productivity, of ice baths and billionaires, all that superstitious Puritan brimstone recycled into plastic morality.

Non fui fui non sum non curo
I was not I was I am not I don't care
How's the sun? Unplug my why or where …

XXV

We were sitting in Dieter's studio, and he was working on the picture, scowling and preoccupied, looking at me as if my head were a kind of problem. I liked it when he got lost like that, because it gave me an opportunity to study him as well, his East German earnestness and the ironic, almost physically concrete pessimism in his way of doing things. Everything about him was heavy. His eyebrows and the thick skin on his forehead. His ponderous movements and exasperated sighs. Sometimes he reminded me of a bipedal tortoise. We'd sit there staring intently at each other but without eye contact, each an object of the other's contemplation. Sometimes silence. Sometimes conversation.

"I was reading this guy, Thucydides," he said. "You probably know about him. The Greek history guy. The part about the disease in Athens. The Pest. What do you call it in English?"

"The plague."

"Ja, the plague. How everybody was thinking they will die any day, so there's no values anymore. No shame. No religion. It's meaningless. People just doing whatever they want, to enjoy something before they get sick, but not with any fun. Just because there's nothing else to do. No tomorrow. You know this?"

"Of course," I said. "It's really famous."

"Yeah. It's really good. No more proper funerals, people burning dead bodies on top of each other, throwing their own dead onto the fires of other people because they don't bother to make a new fire. Just fuck it and walk away. He's dead anyway. Who cares? Nihilismus. He says the people were dying like animals. I think it means they watched each other die like they were watching animals die. Not really caring. Like how many deaths can you see? Life is cheap. Like pigs in the garbage. Or a pile of fish."

"Yeah," I said. "That's pretty much it."

"But I like this idea that they're seeing their religion disproved, right in front of their eyes. There's nothing to pray to to save you from dying. Only statues. Pieces of stone. The temples full of rotten bodies of homeless people who died there, and no one takes them away. No garbage men anymore. Nothing sacred or profane. Their world is over."

He got quiet again and sank back into the painting. I wasn't sure if he expected me to answer.

"I don't know," I said. "Seems like a very post-imperial, end-is-near kind of feeling. I feel that way sometimes, but then I wonder if it isn't just me. Like the pessimism is in my own eyes. Like that saying when a thief looks at a saint, all he sees are his pockets, you know? Maybe I'm missing the point. I don't have any children. I'm starting to rot. Thinking about dead elephants and terrorism, instead of something positive. Maybe kids give you something to live for and have a little hope. And every age has its disgruntled crackpots who think the world's about to end in some cataclysm, the Apocalypse, the Black Death, the Bomb, Y2K, the Pandemic, and it hasn't. That's something to keep in mind. I think it's a kind of vanity. Like we're so special, we have to be destroyed. Not just another generation of animals or a year's worth of leaves. But then it always turns out that's just what we were. Just different mouths saying the same old shit in one book or song after another."

"Ja, sure. But that's not what I mean. I mean this plague idea. To give a shit about nothing. That is the plague. The new plague. Not the symptom. The sickness. Like you said, the sickness can be in the eyes. I have sick eyes. I look and see nothing. An empty shitty world where some people are lucky and comfortable and everybody else is living like slaves. Or the refugees. And I'm doing what I want because there's nothing else to do. Paint some useless pictures. Drink, smoke, die. Whatever."

I laughed. "Now you're making me feel like an optimist."

"Hey, man. I'm sorry. It's close to the time that Lina died, and sometimes I'm getting like this. I start to remember and think about everything again. All the pictures, the blood, the gummy bear. I get depressed. So, it's weird because the negative ideas become more persuasive at this time. Like they're more true. Again, the sick eyes. Or maybe I'm getting like the guy Klaus I told you about, brooding over all the death, all the blood of the dead and the ashes of Jews in the water. Getting paranoid. Maybe I should go to the psychiatrist and get some pills like him, be a fat guy with some tits but not depressed anymore. No more thinking about suicide. But I don't like it. I like that even less. It seems like chemical castration, or like a gorilla in the zoo. What do you do? Just sit there with your new tits eating bananas and picking your nose? Watch TV? Is that an improvement? But I'm not a child molester, I'm a painter. Why do I need to be castrated? Maybe both are no good. Ach, now I am just talking shit. I should just shut up. Put my head in the bag. Turn on the gas. Like Bernard Buffet. Then they find me naked, all rotten and bubbling, with my head in a bag and a paint brush up my ass like a thermometer. *Decomposition of the Molester*. Mixed media. Then put me in a tank of form-aldehyde and make some postcards."

"Well, I don't know if these really are times like those, but in times like those even aristocrats committed suicide. Phi-losophers and artists too. If you're thinking like that and you like Thucydides, you should read Tacitus. There are some great suicides in there. The philosopher Seneca. Or Petronius, the guy who wrote the *Satyricon*. Nero didn't like him anymore, so Petronius killed himself to avoid a phony prosecution and some humiliating form of execution. But he made a party out of it, had his friends over for dinner and slowly died while they drank up his best booze and told dirty jokes and listened to music. No serious topics allowed, no philosophy, no clichés about Socrates or Cato. Can you imagine a party like that? Your friend's suicide bash. And he's perfectly healthy."

"Wow. How did he do it?"

"I didn't want to say, but he slit his wrists open. That was the upper-class way to go. Hanging yourself or jumping off aqueducts was strictly for the poor. No one cared if they killed themselves. But upper-class guys would have a doctor cut them open. So Petronius had his wrists slit, then wrapped them up, and throughout the evening he untied and retied the bandages, flooding and clotting the wounds to prolong the time it would take him to die so he could hang out a little longer. Then he sent an insulting letter to Nero, listing all the perverted shit the emperor did and the prostitutes and high-society sluts he did it with—all the golden showers and felching with Vestal Virgins and children, that kind of stuff. But it seems like there was an attitude of joy and satire, at least the way Tacitus describes it. A totally aristocratic fuck you, I'm out of here. You're the emperor of the end of the world, you fat piece of shit. And by the way, your poetry is shit too.

"It's in the *Annals*. There was another guy named Thrasea Paetus who also slashed his wrists and told Nero to fuck off. The *Annals* didn't survive complete, and that's the last scene in the book as it comes down to us. It breaks off with Thrasea waving his bleeding arms around and splashing blood on the floor as a libation to Jupiter the Liberator. He turns to say something to his friend Demetrius, a cynic philosopher, and just like that the book stops and trails off into oblivion. Dot,

dot, dot. Who knows what he would have said? Something very dark and dry, as a living epitaph, but even so it's a great accidental ending."

Mission Statement

Heresy Press promotes freedom, honesty, openness, dissent, and real diversity in all of its manifestations. We discourage authors from descending into self-censorship, we don't blink at alleged acts of cultural appropriation, and we won't pander to the presumed sensitivities of hypothetical readers. We also don't judge works based on the author's age, gender identity, racial affiliation, political orientation, culture, religion, non-religion, or cancellation status. Heresy Press's ultimate commitment is to enduring quality standards, i.e. literary merit, originality, relevance, courage, humor, and aesthetic appeal.

Newsletter

Don't miss the Heresy Press newsletter SPEAKEASY:
https://heresy-press.com/newsletter

Other Heresy Press Titles

Nothing Sacred: Outspoken Voices in Contemporary Fiction
edited by Bernard Schweizer & James Morrow
The Hermit by Katerina Grishakova
Deadpan by Richard Walter
Unsettled States by Tom Casey
Devil Take It by Daniel Debs Nossiter